THE ROADS AROUND PERDIDO

Other writings by Joseph M. Ferguson, Jr.

The Summerfield Stories. Fort Worth: Texas Christian University Press, 1985
Westering. Portland, Oregon: Inkwater Press, 2010

Acknowledgments:

For the return of publishing rights the author extends his thanks to the following periodicals where some of these stories first appeared: *Glimmer Train* ("Gleanings"); *Short Story* ("The Eighth World of Royden Taul" and "The Westward Inn"); *South Dakota Review* ("Family Album"); *The Pawn Review* ("Fool's Paradise" under the title of "The Downhill Geezer"); and *Pleiades* ("Report on the Hadleyburg Renaissance"). Thanks also to Inkwater Press, Portland Oregon, for kind encouragement and permissions granted.

THE ROADS AROUND PERDIDO
Stories

Joseph M. Ferguson, Jr.

SUNSTONE
PRESS

SANTA FE

Sunstone books may be purchased for educational, business, or sales promotional use. For information please write: Special Markets Department, Sunstone Press, P.O. Box 2321, Santa Fe, New Mexico 87504-2321.
Book and cover design > R. Ahl
Cover art > Sandra Lea Quinlan
Printed on acid-free paper

Library of Congress Cataloging-in-Publication Data

Names: Ferguson, J. M. (Joseph M.), author.
Title: The roads around Perdido : stories / Joseph M. Ferguson, Jr.
Description: Santa Fe : Sunstone Press, [2019] | Summary: "A collection of
    ten related stories set largely in the American Southwest from
    mid-twentieth century to the present"-- Provided by publisher.
Identifiers: LCCN 2019023388 (print) | LCCN 2019023389 (ebook) | ISBN
    9781632932693 (paperback ; acid-free paper) | ISBN 9781611395778 (ebook)

Classification: LCC PS3556.E713 A6 2019 (print) | LCC PS3556.E713 (ebook)
    | DDC 813/.54--dc23
LC record available at https://lccn.loc.gov/2019023388

LC ebook record available at https://lccn.loc.gov/2019023389

WWW.SUNSTONEPRESS.COM
SUNSTONE PRESS / POST OFFICE BOX 2321 / SANTA FE, NM 87504-2321 /USA
(505) 988-4418 / ORDERS ONLY (800) 243-5644 / FAX (505) 988-1025

Dedication

To the memory of my parents,
my first good fortune in life,
Margaret Elizabeth McAlister
(1912–1993)
and
Joseph Martin Ferguson
(1909–1981)

"From the top of Lost Hill, legend had it that you could see into the next state. But there was always a haze on the horizon as though you looked toward other places from somewhere outside of time. Perhaps that was because it was the Lost Country or only that we were very young."

—"The Lost Country," from *The Lost Notebooks of Loren Eiseley*

Contents

Preface

The ten stories in the *The Roads Around Perdido* were written over the last three decades. I had just turned fifty when I began, and my first book, *The Summerfield Stories*, had just been published. A reviewer referred to Summerfield, one of the two main characters, as a "doppleganger." By then I had read Dostoyevsky's short novel, *The Double*, and I was pleased that he noticed.

I owe my reading habit to my great good fortune in acquiring a memorable professor for my freshman advisor when I registered at the University of New Mexico. He put me in his English class. Early on, he asked us to write a short composition about our ambitions. At the end of his written comment about my response he closed with what seems to me even now irrefutable insight: "To write," he advised, "you must just read." I was reading constantly after that—slowly, of course, and still am.

When I went to his office one day to tell him I had just read Maugham's *Of Human Bondage*, a novel high on his reading list, he sat me down and began by fixing me in his gaze and correcting me: "You don't mean you read it—you mean you lived it." I have forgotten what else transpired, but in that living moment I knew he was right.

But as for living a work of fiction, how ever could a would-be author create such a thing? To this daunting question I was also gifted with an answer some two years later, this time from a visiting professor who was also a writer of some reputation, offering a course in fiction writing in the summer session before my senior year. It must have been a question which haunted many of us, for when it arose we were all poised for his answer. "Where do we get our subject matter," someone had asked. "What shall we write about?" He paused and smiled to himself, as if glad to respond. "A writer writes," he replied, "what he or she feels compelled to write about." "But of course!" I thought, and I won't forget that simple, liberating answer. Whenever in doubt I've returned to it, renewed.

Since I turned forty-four I've spent my years in Paradise, so to speak. I refer to the traveling job I stumbled upon which never seemed anything like work. Instead, I set my own itinerary, keeping to the back roads whenever I could, crossing back and forth over that part of the earth I belonged to, the American Southwest where I grew up. The roads I loved most were those in northeastern New Mexico, where I discovered—imagined, rather—the ghost town of Perdido (Spanish for "Lost," of course), and adjoining southeastern Colorado, where I describe in the title story the road south out of La Junta. Traffic was sparse over those roads. When you crossed the Canadian River canyon between Wagon Mound and Roy you were all by yourself, save for the earth and sky you were part of, and then, that feeling of coming to the end of your road where one of the little towns with an inn was waiting in the darkness for you. Yes, I felt compelled to write about it, and slowly I did, keeping a notebook always handy.

By the time I had five or six stories I began to think about finding the right order for them, and after staring at them for a while they fell irreversibly into place without any trouble at all—amazing, it seemed. Thus I'll urge they be read in order, and I'll caution readers they might encounter somewhere in there another doppleganger.

The story I like best wanders the most (I call that "the beauty of indirection"), and I wasn't sure, at several junctions, that I was going to be able to finish it, but when I finally did it was as if the ending had been there waiting for me all along. It's likely the best story I ever wrote. It's also the only one I ever wrote in the present tense. Could be, when I come to think about it, I should try that again sometime.

Youth

Summers we went west. Out on the plains we'd come across the baked clay beds of vanished rivers bearing names like Smokey Hill and Arikaree, with retinues of cottonwood and willow left to trace their course. We'd keep whenever we could to the back roads, and the little towns we'd see, lost but in the distance shimmering still, were like the Cities of Cibola to us, and we their first explorers. At the end of our road, if ever we made it that far, lay my small city by the sea, but we were young back then, and never in any hurry. Not us.

Once, on those same high plains, to see a town we had always missed we had to go out of our way—but then not really, since really we had no way. It was the end of a spring that had been delayed by a strenuous winter, but the sun shone down on our vacant highway where a gentle wind was blowing warm, and at the edge of town as we arrived a field was floating white with wild daisies. The people we saw had dressed as if the weather might still go either way, but all were smiling, and a state of subdued elation was everywhere.

Not that there were all that many to be seen—a woman in a light blue cardigan who had just stepped out of a bakery, pausing to look around, with a sack of something in her hand, a man in heavy coveralls who had paused for a smoke where the door to his sun-lit garage stood open, a man in a tan topcoat, tipping his hat and holding open the door to a bank for a white-haired lady while she inched in first. There wasn't even a place to buy gas, which we were low on, save for a truck stop a mile west of town at a junction with a road that came down from the north. There were two or three places to eat, but we settled for circling around a couple of times on the brick side streets, it being only mid-morning. Our windows were down, and I won't forget the damp odor of the earth loosened up, or the way the mechanic in coveralls nodded and lifted his free hand to wave as we passed—the way everyone in town was smiling, to each other or to themselves. When you hit a town right, there are always things you remember.

As for places to eat, there were, with luck, some good ones to be stumbled upon. For lunch, there might be the small cafe near the middle of town, with a wood floor, say, and a brick front with a big window looking out on the street. There, never having put away childish things, we might be sitting contentedly over hamburgers and cokes. "Why, this is heaven," I might sigh, to which our waitress might smile, yet not without a touch of wonder on her face.

At evening, once, in a town on the grasslands not far from the Great Divide, we were in just such a place for our supper. Through the propped open door came the scent of the grass and the song of the meadowlark out beyond, but our moment of heaven was broken by a sidewalk disturbance which at the time seemed quite remarkable—a kid on a skateboard clattering by. Even so, this small misfortune was soon redeemed by the arrival of some memorable company. A battered pickup rattled up to the curb and a bone-tired cowboy emerged to drag himself to a nearby table. He gave only brief consideration to the menu handed him, folded it up, flexed his hands slowly and then laid them to rest in his lap. While he sat contemplating the window it occurred to me that he might have been younger than he looked. I heard him order a hamburger steak.

His order was shortly ready, but just as the waitress approached both were distracted by a sudden commotion outside. The skateboarder, making another pass, had gone down in a heap, and the plate glass window shivered. We heard him let slip an oath or two before slinking off in the night, and for one long moment the cowboy and the waitress seemed to regard one another. Then, straightening himself, the man summoned the strength to speak the few crisp words that were doubtless his last for a day that had doubtless been short on them.

"Break your neck," he pronounced, and then to the plate set before him he surrendered his lackluster attention.

But as for heaven, in search of my small city, in a later year, we did make it all the way to the sea. And we did find cities there, though not, of course, the one we were looking for, the one by itself on a plain beside that sea—the one of my imagination, I now acknowledge. It lives there still, though I doubt I'll ever have all the details. Only that its streets trail off to nowhere on the plain or disappear in the sand of the beach, while the traffic on them is non-existent, save for a bicycle now and then pedaled softly by, and the sidewalks, strolled only by a few unhurried pedestrians, are never teeming. Its buildings are white, sun-bleached, with its citizens inhabiting the upstairs flats without clamor or rancor, and late in the afternoons when the sun takes a downward turn way out over the sea and the incoming breeze is at play with the curtains parted at their windows, they are entranced by the light that falls on floors, on walls, and on each other's faces. In the stealth of the hours that follow it is impossible for them to tell where daylight ends and darkness begins.

Later that same year, an unmistakable darkness was gathering as we strayed into a village in the juniper hills just beyond the great rift which runs along the spur of the Rockies. It was getting late in the year for us to be out on the road. Gold leaves from the cottonwoods were down in the streets, and under the town's few hanging streetlamps we could see wisps of smoke or haze adrift. Nothing at all was stirring, but in some of the small dark houses along the way the lights had gone on in kitchen windows. For almost a mile the highway on which we entered became the main street, and in a lighted window close beside the end of it, with shoulders hunched beneath a contemplative gaze, an elderly woman was sitting alone, raising a spoon to her lips.

If I'm not mistaken, it was my first wife who was beside me in the passenger seat at the time, and I still hear those cautionary whisperings with which she countered whenever my mood turned somber. "Oh Graves," she used to warn, "you're drifting." She was a decent sort, I like to think, though I could never be sure just what she thought of me. "Oh Charles," she used to say sometimes, "you can be funny when you want," as if to be entertained were all that mattered in life. Still, I can't say how, but I knew even then that she was the only wife I was ever going to have.

Family Album

I

On the interstate, making his way past Pueblo, he caught sight of the college on the hill and thought of the home they had left behind. It was neither the first nor the last, as it happened, and it had happened, he suspected, on that spring day when as a young man he had driven across that slow descent of prairie to a town in western Kansas for an interview with another college. Its friendliness, its clean brick streets, its greenness in May had enchanted him, but he had at first refused their offer, knowing his wife and sons to be happily settled where they were. There had been rain showers as he returned, and the sky, hazy above that vast and undulating green midsection of the continent, blushed softly with rosy light. He had heard the meadowlarks calling, and the air had been scented with wildflowers. In the end he had not been able to resist moving again, and later, when the opportunity presented itself, he had taken a further step and left his teaching position for the traveling job. When he had been at it a year he had known that he would never be able to do anything else.

Now it was four o'clock at the onset of October, and having cleared the pass called La Veta, he was descending the long narrow valley of Sangre de Cristo Creek in time to see afternoon shadows dancing, leaf-shaped, in the gentle wind, running along the crumpled walls of a forgotten shed as if the wind were visible, one persistent current at work in the fields and forests that might have told him, had he been less preoccupied, that the earth remained alive in all of its parts, stirring in that lovely autumn light.

Finally, when it was almost too late, he pulled over and stopped at a place where the graveled shoulder widened, got out, and made his way slowly down the embankment on the opposite side of the highway toward the creek. Pushing his way through tangled brush and willow, he reached the water, swift and clear in its channel, deeper here near the bottom of the valley than he had expected.

Stooping, he bathed his face in the cold and incoherent water, then straightened to search the cloudless sky. He had intended to say some kind of prayer, but he found no words for uttering beyond that expression of spontaneous denial which had escaped him and drummed in his consciousness since his wife had called—even though he had somehow known the truth before she told him. He repeated the gesture, but again he stood helpless and silent. Turning at last, he toiled slowly up the embankment, making the top just in time to receive a warning blast from the horn of a semi-truck as it rounded the bend in the highway above him.

II

When his brother had died he had come home from the university, and he had discovered that in his grief he still felt concern for his father, a thousand miles away in Wyoming when his mother had reached him. His grandparents had come, and friends and neighbors had been coming and going, one of them bringing a minister who had finally gotten his mother to kneel while he placed his hand on her head and prayed—"I can't do it," his mother had protested, "why won't you just leave me alone." He had waited into the night, no longer heeding their various condolences, listening instead for the sound of his father's car in the driveway and wondering how he, his oldest son, should greet him, knowing neither how to say all that he felt nor all that he would feel when he saw him. When at last he had heard him and gone to the door to see his father moving heavily toward him through the darkness, he had just stood there holding the screen door open for him and staring into his infinitely weary face. Yet there had been only a moment's hesitation before he had felt his father's arms around him and, to his profound relief, himself returning his embrace, just as someone—it was not his mother but perhaps his grandmother—someone who had come up behind him in the house gave out a long, low moan releasing sorrow, pain, and longing. He had not known for certain who it was because everyone had come forward to receive his father, but he had known he would not forget that moaning sigh so sympathetic that it was as if the sound had been wrung from his own heart.

Now he had come late to his brother's memorial service, not wanting to sit with his parents, feeling an old resentment. He wondered if they knew that their quarrel, whatever its source, had entangled and harmed them all, that it had been a worry to his brother also, that while he lived they had more than once confided their concern to one another.

He watched them both, sitting there in the front pew with Tim between them, waiting for the minister to bring the service to a close. His father's head was slightly bowed, but he still saw the bald spot showing where the hair used to part behind the crest of his skull. He had seen his shoulders start to shake while he listened to Paul, his brother's friend who had introduced him to the church. It was Paul, he had known already, who had once found his brother half conscious on the floor of the projection booth at the theater where they both worked, but he doubted that his father had known about the incident until now, for he doubted that his mother, who would have known, had told him.

Now they were all standing and praying, and when they reached "amen" he looked up and saw people hesitating, then some of them beginning to gravitate toward the front to speak to his parents. He started to join them, but then he stopped, not far behind his father, whom he saw turning from the minister and reaching for the hand of Paul.

"Paul, that was beautiful," his father said hoarsely. "I'm just so proud of him..." he began, but then his voice broke and his head fell forward on Paul's shoulder. With an effort he tried again: "I'm so proud of him for having a friend like you," he said weakly, and then they embraced again. He noticed that Paul, always composed, had turned a little pale.

A little later, outside in the fine October light, he found himself on the fringe of those who lingered on the lawn and the church steps when his parents emerged. His mother had her arm in his father's, and the two of them stood just outside the vestibule, blinking in the sunlight. Then one of them dropped something—a set of keys, it sounded like—and for a long moment everyone hesitated again, as if spellbound by the sound of the keys on the concrete steps. Then his father, looking weary and old, turned and bent, still holding his mother's arm, and retrieved the keys with his free hand. Something about the gesture, something about the angle of his father's jaw and cheekbone as he straightened himself and inclined his face slightly toward the sun, deflected his own hard gaze, dissolving in him for the moment this resentment toward his parents which he did not himself quite understand.

III

The photographs had never been collected in a family album like the one he had sometimes looked through when he was a boy, yet they existed, tossed carelessly into a couple of large manila envelopes and stored in a cardboard box. Often neglected, the collection had not been added to in recent years, but he knew that it contained, up to a point, the record of their lives together when sorted with care by someone such as himself. One afternoon when he was alone in the house, he located the box and got it down from the dark and dusty corner of a closet shelf.

Immediately, he was absorbed. Had he forgotten what was there to be so plainly seen? Looking for his lost son, he came across what appeared to be a professional portrait of Loren, his oldest, probably taken at school at about the second grade. His hair was fine and light and long but neatly trimmed, and how delicate the bone work of his jaw and chin seemed. He had observed the trait in all three of his sons, though no one had ever remarked upon it, and it was not something he had looked for, but rather recognized, having seen it in his father. He was smiling radiantly with flushed cheeks, and yet, at the same time, there seemed to emanate from this same countenance an aura of sadness which he, the father, could detect but not explain. Did life do this to youth so soon, he wondered, or was it the case with his sons only? The longer he looked the more he began to perceive. Perhaps people did not look closely enough, and perhaps that was just as well. It crossed his mind to proceed no further.

But then there was his wife. He held her now two years before he had met her—the photograph was dated 1954, which must have been her eighteenth year. She sat on a beach in a one-piece bathing suit, the sky hazy but luminous behind her—it was the shore of Lake Michigan, she had once told him, not far from her home. She sat facing the camera, calves and feet folded under her, where the water met the sand, and her arms, just slightly double-jointed at the elbow, were thrown outward and skyward—a Marilyn Monroe kind of pose, he thought, though she seemed to him a prettier girl than Marilyn Monroe had been. She had at that time of her life Monroe's blond hair, a lock of it falling over her tilted face as she fixed her gaze, as if sighting with her extended left arm, toward that softly luminous sky. She was smiling then. She was eighteen, her hands open to the sky, and glad of life.

He turned his attention to a photograph he had taken of her as she cradled Tim, then near his first birthday, on an outing in St. Vrain Canyon, near Longmont. It was their first autumn in Colorado, and her face, cast down toward Tim's, worked in him a pang of wonder. Over the years her hair had darkened, and she had tried several styles of wearing it, yet here in her thirty-first year she appeared suddenly unaffected, known and yet forgotten, so that he was stunned by what he now beheld. Her hair was by then dark brown with a wave of it sweeping naturally over her forehead. Her features were fine, sensitive, serious, and touched by that same shadow of sadness he had detected in Loren's portrait—but a sadness less bewildered, more resigned. She was, to state it plainly, a beautiful woman, and this was surely the prime of her life—perhaps the prime of both their lives, unnoticed by either of them. But no, he could be mistaken: perhaps the very consciousness of something of the sort had brought about that sad knowledge, that hint of shadow to the beautiful face recorded before him.

His reverie drifted toward a time when he was little more than a child.

"When we came in from our walk, Charlie," his father was saying that long ago evening, "you and Wallace were stretched out on the bed side by side, and I couldn't help pointing out to your mother that you were almost as long as Wallace." He spoke happily and not without pride even if what he had said was an exaggeration (his uncle, like his father, being six feet tall, while he himself was just beginning his twelfth year—he knew because it was the summer after the war had ended).

Odd, the things the memory chose to keep. They had been in the midst of a vacation, the first that he could remember, and they were traveling out west. With them was Wallace, youngest of his father's three older brothers, the uncle who, after serving in Europe during the war, had come home to teach at the high school where his father had been teaching and coaching.

And he had always harbored a dim recollection of the motel room in Kansas where he and his uncle had been napping after the long summer day of crossing the plains. When his mother and father had come in from their walk he had stirred half awake to see their shadowy forms through the doorway opened on the dusky adjoining room, to hear their soft voices, also shadowy like the fading light in the room. And even then, he reflected, at the time when he may have been forming his love of the road and when his parents and his uncle must have been enjoying the prime of their lives together, he might have glimpsed how all things pass and most fade from memory—but not, somehow, this.

Gathering the contents of the envelopes, then hesitating, he decided to look for a portrait of Will, and his search yielded a small, wallet-sized print that looked as though it might have been done at his high school, perhaps around his sixteenth year. His face, plump in his childhood but thinner now, was inclined just slightly toward the right, while his auburn hair was swept toward the left of his forehead. His lips were thin, but his smile generous. It was the eyes which gave him pause. The eyes seemed wistful, preoccupied or not quite focused, as though perceiving something distant and unremarked. It was as if the knowledge of his mortality had been ever present, even then, and he understood more clearly his son's need to leave home during his last year in school, embracing thus at least a little of the life that he would never know fully. Still, he wondered at his need to keep his symptoms to himself almost until the end. Learning of them, his wife had sought the opinion of a specialist down in Phoenix, and there, as the doctor informed him of his true condition, she was made to witness his response, the sudden pallor and the involuntary trembling and shortness of breath, nothing more, and she alone was there to take him in her arms and hold him close.

For he himself had not been present, but away on the road, and so depended for the image he retained on her recounting voice, fading, at the end, to a desperate and barely audible whisper. Born of this image once removed and spread, he knew, among the four survivors closest to the one now lost, the ghost, it may have been, of what his son for years had borne alone, his pain seemed palpable and finely honed, though time, he also knew, would come to dull it, and yet he sensed that it was destined to be long in lingering, and never, perhaps, to wholly heal.

IV

They had married much too young, she often thought, and for years she had doubted that he loved her. In the early years she had often accused him of as much, but later she had let the subject drop, gradually cultivating a reserve intended to match his own, even though in the end she had surpassed him.

From the beginning he had alluded to his desire to write, and it was true that the stories had begun to come when he gave up teaching, little bursts of quaint imaginings—something unfinished about a "Hadleyburg Renaissance," something about a "Westward Inn," an oasis in the sunbelt which seemed to cater to some downtrodden seniors. He sometimes forced these upon her, hoping for praise, she knew, though she had none to offer. With foolish expectations he sent out his manuscripts, and she saw them come back in their sad manila envelopes, looking lonely and rejected. Then, after a lapse, appeared one which she took upon herself to read, alone, and which she re-read. It had something to do with a nebulous "Eighth World" which awaited its realization, the invention of a charlatan, it seemed to her, and yet there was such a buoyant manner in the telling of it that she found her spirits lifted, and she considered that she might tell him sometime, when the moment was right, that she thought it better than the rest.

But as the years passed she was left to assume that he had abandoned his creative impulse. In its place he had succumbed to what seemed to her a compulsive pessimism, infecting, she knew, not only herself but their children, so that she was glad when he was gone most of the time, and had been glad also for the company of Will, her second son, while she had it, since what she had loved most about him was his joy in life, his dauntless goodwill and resilience—how different he was from Loren, who was his father's son, or, for that matter, how little he had in common with his father, who, she was sure, had appreciated him not at all.

Now she had her own career, and, never a good provider, he seemed to falter as she succeeded. There were months, she knew, when he earned barely enough commission from his textbook job to pay his travel expenses. He had accused her more than once of having always been competitive with him, but one evening as their anniversary approached—their twenty-fourth, as she calculated—she found his conversation taking a conciliatory turn.

"You know, Hadley," he volunteered, "I've now been married half my life, and you're the only woman I've ever had anything to do with." He seemed pleased with this remarkable finding, cited as if in evidence of a rare devotion. Thinking about it, she discerned that his claim was probably the truth, but offered less for her reassurance than for his own.

"That ought to count for something with you," he added. There was such satisfaction in his pronouncement that she brought her thoughts to the surface.

"You're in love with yourself, Charles. Always have been."

He let the subject drop after that and lapsed into a sullen silence, but then one night he asked her to kindly elaborate on what she meant. She tried to explain that he was selfish, had always been—no, not that he was not a generous man in some respects, as generous as his modest circumstances permitted—but selfish with himself in some way that she despaired of ever making him understand. And then, incensed by his anger as he demanded that she explain herself, her own animosity and grief surged uncontrollably, and again she uttered aloud what she had only barely conceived, dredged from some sunless depth of her heart, "I wish to God that you had died instead."

And now, she knew, their lives ebbed on with old resentment, kept silenced, for the time being, with new reserve.

V

The trail began by crossing a broad meadow which the city had incorporated for a park—a dry meadow, to be sure, but waving with grasses and weeds, many of the latter tall and in flower beside the path of red volcanic cinder where it cut through and headed straight for the mountains. A scattering of ponderosa pine, growing thicker and turning to forest in the distance, seemed just enough to lend perspective to the view of the otherwise open fields that surrounded the hiker on this first mile of journey. It was the first day of summer, it occurred to him, the day of the solstice, and the mingled smells of the grasses and weeds—was it ragweed that he detected among them—at this early hour reminded him vaguely of summer mornings long ago and far away.

It was hard for him to realize that all this time there had been a trail so close to his home. Not that it was within walking distance, exactly, but much closer than the one on the other side of town that he sometimes drove to. He had been told that there were trails all over the Dry Hills area, but he had paid little heed and had almost forgotten, and now he was happily surprised to find that one of them—one that led to a high park in the nearest mountain—was so accessible to him.

He wondered, in fact, whether this day was not the fulfillment of a dream—dream or reality, he could never determine which, although if it was real he was sure he had dreamed about it too—a dream of a place he had harbored half-consciously since the days when they had lived in Reno, where they had moved when Will was still an infant. Will had spent his first two years there. On autumn weekends, and again late in the spring when the winter had finally spent itself, they took happily spontaneous trips northwest out of Reno to a lonely and lovely country, the backside of Northern California, forgotten, almost, at least on the roads they found to travel, where a village called Sierraville and another called Portola had become their stopping points, and where somewhere in that dreamlike country an even lesser road forked to the right and headed into some low-lying and neglected mountains, green with timber and meadows and alder-lined trout streams, a place that they had stumbled upon just once, it seemed to him, and that he had never had the chance to fully explore.

Now, again, he had that sense of exploring mountains which seemed, at least to him on this particular morning, new and neglected. There were two other cars in the parking lot when he arrived, but he suspected that those might belong to joggers who were busy on the loop which, according to the map posted at the trailhead, circled the dry meadow. As far as he could see he had the trail that cut straight through and headed into the foothills all to himself. He hoped it would be that way.

By mid-morning his wish held good. Off to his left in the distance he had heard a dog barking, and the trail had dipped and wound in that direction, but the noise had ceased, and he had seen nothing but some tracks in the trail which had turned from cinder to dust. The breeze that had made the grass and flowers wave and caused his eyes to tear when he crossed the meadow had subsided now, and the day was warming. He had made his way through a patchwork of sunlight and shadow as the sun worked its way above the mountains and appeared now sporadically among pine and spruce, above great granite boulders, and amidst the leaves of occasional aspen and Gambel oak.

Twice he paused to listen to birdsong. There had been the barking of the dog and there was, too, the intermittent rustling of leaves and the soft plodding of his own footsteps and the whispering sounds of his own breathing, beginning to labor rhythmically now as he passed the midpoint of his climbing, but otherwise he had walked in silence. He stopped in his tracks when he heard it, a tinkling, silvery refrain, repeated twice more at intervals, piercing the mid-morning serenity so delicately that it seemed like silence itself. He always listened to the birds at home, but this was a trilling he had never heard before, unreal, unearthly. Yet it had substance, too, a kind of resonance to it, enhanced perhaps by an echo, coming as it did from some distance away and below him, rising from the small, funnel-like valley that he looked down on now, wrapped in the unbrokenly wooded and sunlit mountainsides. Half a mile further, as if to confirm its reality, the refrain brought him to a second stop. Probably not the same bird, he thought, though surely the same species. Some small, shy bird, he considered, given the delicacy of the singing. Perhaps it was similar to the canyon wren he had often heard but seldom seen, except that the canyon wren had something mournful in its caroling. But the song of this bird was unmistakably sweetness and joy, and he knew that it was unlikely he would ever see it, that it would remain, casting upon that wilderness its pure-hearted song, the disembodied voice of the morning light.

The trail was steeper now as it ascended the mountainside where ponderosa pine gave way increasingly to fir and spruce, and he labored a little more slowly toward the clearing called Six Mile Park, the destination he had set for himself, his mind occupied now with other disembodied voices.

Auditory illusions, he had taken to calling them. Almost always it was the same voice he heard, speaking to him softly in the late evening or early morning hours or just as he woke from a dream in one or another of the countless motel rooms he had inhabited, a voice so real and palpable that he would sit up in bed and search the dim room for its source. He had never spoken to her about it, but it was the voice of his wife, the half-spoken, half-whispered single syllable of his name, "Charles, Charles," imprinted no doubt indelibly on his memory from the many times she had addressed him just so in reality, and called up almost eerily then in the predawn hours when he was alone and often far away. He pondered the meaning of these occurrences. Was there something, he wondered, something of considerable weight and import, that he failed to recognize and heed, for always that disembodied voice, though almost whispered, carried a sense of urgency and warning. And there was the sense, too, that even though it was clearly the voice of his wife, it was also in some small but undeniable part the voice of his own conscience.

And there had also been another instance, a singular, chance encounter involving another voice, a voice that was, strangely, both disembodied and embodied. Late in the summer following his son's death, it had spoken to him in clear and simple words, yet he had not immediately grasped their full significance.

It happened on a lonely road in western Minnesota, while he was returning home from Minneapolis and his company's annual meeting, keeping to the back roads as was his habit, feeling discouraged and alienated, as company meetings inevitably left him feeling. He topped a hill and found his way blocked by a stalled and elderly black Buick, an elderly lady standing idly beside it. He could see the car sagging where its left rear tire had shed its worn-out tread. He was glad for the opportunity to make himself useful, to be of some help in the world, and he felt better with himself after he had eased the car to the roadside—"the first thing to do," he admonished her gently, proceeding with the stiffness and tenderness of a man who was himself feeling his years—and changed the tire for her, replacing the ruined one with a spare that did not look much better. Her home, it turned out, was in a small town some twenty miles away.

"You'll be okay then, Ma'am, if you just drive slowly, but be sure to have that tire replaced as soon as you can."

She was tall but a little bent, for the years had begun to wither both body and face, where decades of Minnesota winters were written. Still, she was not unbecoming, and her eyes, both wise and warm, fixed him as if she knew him intimately from his few words and actions, as if she had in those few minutes acquired complete and sympathetic understanding—more, as if she saw him more clearly than he saw himself and wanted to speak to him about it. Yet, excepting her expressions of gratitude, she did not speak until just as he made ready to depart, when she gathered herself to speak those few words, her gift, as it were, as if she hoped it might lodge in his heart forever. "I love you," she said.

He followed her slowly along the highway for a few miles until she turned off on the road to her home. He waved a final goodbye, then sped up again to resume his lonely journey, pondering the meaning of this chance encounter that was replacing, even as he wondered, the weight of his dejection with something lighter—not hope, exactly, but a kind of gratitude, something perhaps he could best call solace. She had seemed relieved upon his arrival, yet not, somehow, disturbed by her plight, certainly not given to any display of anxiety—it was as if she had been there, at that time and place, for his sake only, though he suspected this impression was probably the work of his stimulated imagination. Yet her final words, that final "I love you," spoken so clearly in a voice that had otherwise been strained with age, had seemed to him in some way incongruous—too natural to be inappropriate, too ingenuous to be surprising longer than a fleeting moment, but startling to him all the same. Simple and sincere, the words seemed to him, and yet transcendent, disembodied.

Another hour had passed when, topping another hill on the now empty road before him, he realized with a rush of insight that the voice he had heard, along with the words it had spoken so seemingly displaced, was a voice he had heard before, speaking those same words, and although he was no subscriber to the supernatural, he identified it now as the voice of his deceased son, who had spoken to him just those words in just that manner—that simple and sincere "I love you"—at the end of a telephone conversation, long distance, from somewhere in the last year of his life, taking him even then by surprise, unaware, so that he had not been able to make the right response, his mind too preoccupied. Hanging up the receiver, realizing too late the significance of those last words, he had thought of dialing his son back immediately, but he had not, and the moment had passed. It seemed to him then that his son had spoken to him again this one last time—no, not through the medium of, but rather in consort with the aged lady who had waited for him on the highway—as if to be sure he had heard him, as if to be sure that he, his father, understood.

He had been climbing now, he realized, without really seeing for a while, a somnambulist, almost, his mind led astray as it often was on his hikes by the persistence of memories that were cherished now beyond reality. What called him back was a glimpse of a human figure, the first of the day, just disappearing from sight where the trail switched back above and well ahead of him, above which, in turn, he discovered the early afternoon thunderclouds which had silently begun to build. He paused to listen, but heard nothing. No birds were singing, and the breeze was dead. Some youth, he thought, for in the brief glimpse he had of the figure, it moved gracefully, light on its feet, making good time. And yet, oddly, he had apparently closed the distance between himself and this other lone hiker, unseen till now, who must have been preceding him on the trail since morning.

Unmistakably, there was a coolness creeping into the air around him, and at almost every turn, he was reminded, one could see great trees that had been damaged or destroyed by lightning. The idea of returning, then and there, crossed his mind, but crossed it briefly, and did not stay. His stronger instinct was to proceed. According to the map he had memorized that morning, he had only another mile, at most, to reach the park he sought. His eyes on the trail, he struck out rhythmically again, a little too eager, perhaps—a little desperate, almost—aware that a new energy from somewhere was pushing him now, no longer feeling the pain in his legs, conscious of the accelerated working of his heart.

Some time later, with the first report of the impending storm, he lifted his face to the sky where darkness and light contended. The thunder seemed muted, though no distant rumbling either, since he had journeyed so near to its source, but rather like mountains moving, shifting, just beyond the ridge of the one he had ascended. In its wake he found himself confronting—too easily, he knew—Six Mile Park, his destination, a seemingly mythical glade encompassed, bowl-like, by the high forest, which thinned enough at the distant edge to afford him the momentary prospect of a fading and various terrain, some undiscovered wilderness, sprawling beyond the mountain's crest where it dipped in a saddle between high peaks. And there in the mottled light beneath a great blue spruce on the far side of the clearing, waiting for him, stood that solitary personage, the beautiful youth, whose face, he knew, would be quizzical and kind and starved with an unfathomable longing, and even as his feet labored furiously and his heart pounded with a huge anticipation, he knew, too, that this lost son would be always beyond his embrace, and that from this sleep, merciful and cruel, he was about to wake.

VI

They arrived late in the afternoon, his father easing the rented Datsun—he pampered the car he used for his business travel and would not take it on the rough dirt roads—down the sloping road to the campground, deserted now as they had hoped it would be. It was a place called Chevelon Crossing where his father had taken him once before during a lonely and troubled adolescence. For as long as he could remember his father and mother had loved him. They had loved each other, too, he was sure, but something had happened. He could not say exactly what or when, but he had often tried to explain it to himself because he loved them both, and he had not known what to do.

"They're ducks, son, wild ducks!" his father had said of the half dozen or so great birds that had taken off from the stream when they approached it on that fall weekend years ago. Later they had sighted them again on the water downstream, and he had seen the red in their heads and in the bands on their wings before they took flight again. He remembered how the sight of them had elated his father, but he remembered even better how his father had tried, with little success, to convey his elation to him, to cheer his youngest son on that camping trip he had insisted they make together.

Now at last, he realized, he was cheered. He had been cheered to see that his father and mother apparently did not mind being the grandparents he felt he had prematurely made them—even if, as his father with granddaughter in arms had taken pride in announcing to the neighbors, it had happened to the day on their thirtieth anniversary. Most of all, though, he was cheered to see that in place of the old rancor there was now what appeared to be a truce between them. Now at last, he also realized, for this one afternoon that they had together, he was alone with his father and with a heart full of things that he wanted to say to him.

His father stopped the Datsun, and they both got out slowly, stretching themselves. He recognized the place, a place where juniper and pine met in the rugged foothill country of the Mogollon Rim, not so high as they might have gone and the stream not so wild, slowed by an unseen dam miles up the winding canyon, but high enough, and best of all abandoned in favor of higher elevations this time of year, the height of summer. Even the ducks were gone, they discovered.

It was hard for him to begin, perhaps because he knew that his father had always found it difficult to speak intimately with him. There had been a time when he had felt that he was his father's favorite, but as the years had passed he had become more distant. Perhaps it had been the same with his brothers. His father had been gone a lot of the time, but when he was home he would sometimes drag him to the courts at the school a block away where, until the sky began to darken, they would drive their tennis balls across the net between them.

"Dad," he began, trying to collect his thoughts, "you were always a good father to me." He saw his father glance at him, then look down and swallow. "I think of all the things I should have done," he said quietly.

"I know, Dad, that you might not think you were," he struggled, "but that's why I want to tell you...to all of us, I mean."

They heard a faint rumbling on the dusty road above them, and looking up they caught glimpses of a cautious pick-up truck at places where the road was exposed to their view. It was coming down through the juniper forest on the road they had turned off from. They heard it rattle on the bridge above the

24

stream and then, shifting gear somewhere beyond it, begin its laboring ascent of the other side of the canyon on its way toward the town of Winslow, a destination it might have determined to reach by nightfall.

In its wake he began to hear things that he had forgotten about, the things that lived there daily, perhaps all the days of their lives. There was a bird of some sort—a canyon wren, his father told him—whose cry resounded off the cliffs across the stream in the deepening afternoon, something remotely like the voice of the loon such as he had heard in Ohio where he lived now, but a shriller song, fainter but more piercing, somehow, with descending, mournful notes at the end of its carol which expired in infinite sadness. So human, it seemed to him. He could not help thinking that this was the ghost of his brother, there beyond the stream at sundown, crying out sadly for his lost life, crying out wanting to join them. Yet maybe it was just the bird crying for the dying day, personifying for him and for his father, who also listened attentively, the sense of loss in their hearts, a sense of loss that encompassed his oldest brother, too, whom the years had estranged from them.

"Dad," he continued, "I've often wished I had your patience, too. I've always admired that in you."

His father looked surprised, but smiled. "I've never thought of myself as a patient man," he said.

A whining sound, higher pitched than that of the pick-up, claimed their attention, and there came into view a motorbike with its rider—a youth, apparently. It, too, crossed the bridge and began its ascent toward the lingering sunset, its single headlamp casting a bouncing and feeble shaft of light before it. The rider seemed somehow more alone in the world than the truck driver, perhaps because more exposed to the oncoming night and the elements, and thrusting his helmeted head, his lean back and shoulders forward over the handlebars, he seemed bound not just for Winslow but the end of the earth, some obscure destination where the last faint streak of aquamarine light was awash against the first night sky.

He felt his father's arm around him, an embrace he gratefully returned. "I love you, son," his father said to him.

VII

The messages which turned up on and then disappeared from his answering machine, seemingly beyond his control, sometimes had the effect of old photographs, forgotten and then reappearing, unannounced.

"Don't forget your ties, you boob," he had called to say to himself, reminding himself on the road while he thought of it that he had left two of his ties at the cleaners for over a month. And later, having forgotten about this reminder but coming across it when he was home again, what gave him pause was not his own voice, always a little strange to him, but the gentle burst of laughter which followed it in the background, her laughter, her voice.

For it was true that he was glad for her company when, lately, she would take off from work occasionally and travel with him. They chose, always, a room with two beds, just as, when together in the home they now had to themselves, they slept at opposite ends of the house. Yet, despite all the times when the old anger had flared and hardened his resolve to be gone when the children were gone, despite the fact that neither of them nor their sons would have predicted it, they had stayed together under the same roof, and both of them, he sensed, were glad they had. Had there been anyone in whom he confided, he might have confessed that yes, in spite of all, it seemed that he and his wife were now friends.

How had it happened, he wondered? There was no turning point that he could put his finger on, but coming amid relapses, too, were certain incidents, fragments of experience which on the surface seemed more often than not the merest trifles, but which left with him a lasting impression.

There had been that day at the beginning of the summer after Tim had left them. Another school year, another year of his travel itinerary had passed, and he had arrived before she was home from work. He had gone to the backyard and stretched out on the recliner that she liked to use for sunbathing. The sun had been shining with the first warmth of the season, but a patch of cloud drifting rapidly overhead had given him a sudden empty sensation which, when coupled with the empty house, had made him realize that they were getting along in years—an involuntary foreknowledge of what his life would be like if she were ever really gone from it.

Toward the end of that summer, unseen behind the gauze curtains covering the kitchen window, he watched her as she wound and coiled a garden hose not far away from him in that same backyard. Her arms seemed weary, beginning to thin from age, and she bent about her task in a curiously mechanical way. When she finished she straightened herself with a faint but audible sigh, and he knew then that he had witnessed a small yet momentous event, an image of his wife that allowed him, for his part, to forgive her everything.

Finally, she had left a message on his answering machine which he had tried to preserve and eventually lost, but not before it had left its enduring mark. He had arrived home to find that she had shampooed the carpeting, and her message explained that she just wanted to test his machine, having bumped its switch box at the baseboard outlet. There was little intimacy about the message, but something about the hesitant, halting rhythm of her voice made him attentive. She seemed self-conscious about picking her words, but then at the end she rushed on without even a comma: "I just wanted to see if it was working alright and I think it is." He had thought that was all, but then, after another hesitation came two final, softly piercing syllables: "Bye, bye." The sound of that departing voice, with its last words so gently ominous, haunted him long after he had lost it, enabling him to glimpse, as it were, the far side of his own soul, where he found that he had, after all, always cared for her.

VIII

She accepted at once his reasoning for his proposal that their vacation, their second since they were alone together, should be to Florida in the midst of the summer, for she found herself relieved by the prospect of confronting the demon that had nagged her for almost three years now, the time that had passed since they had last heard from their first-born son.

"We can do our sightseeing on the way back," he had suggested, and she had agreed, knowing that their time was short and their journey long, knowing that the purpose of their trip, as he had proposed, was to visit Loren, their six-years-married, childless and estranged son, from whose mother-in-law they had obtained an address, though she had no further information to impart to them. Their chances for a successful trip, which she herself would not have thought to propose, seemed highly improbable to her, but he had insisted that since they had a chance it was somehow imperative that they try, that they might never forgive themselves if they didn't at least try to show their son that they cared about him, their long drive east to St. Petersburg in July seemingly the right time and circumstance to reinforce their demonstration of concern. Infected by his sense of urgency, she had known suddenly that he was right and had felt intuitively that they might find Loren and his wife and make their peace in spite of the odds.

And so she submitted quietly while, in the name of efficiency, he drove east out of Flagstaff on the interstate, a route they both despised. She was no help when it came to road maps, and leaving such details to him, she was aware only that he turned south from I-40 somewhere after they crossed the Mississippi and that somewhere in Georgia they stopped at a roadside stand to buy a sack of peaches, intended to be a gift at their hoped-for reunion. She was aware, too, that the heat and humidity and mosquitoes were even more oppressive than she had anticipated.

She closed her eyes and dozed when she could, sometimes opening them to find her attention given to the faint sound and reflection of the key chain dangling from the ignition. She had noticed her increasing perception of such small and inconsequential appearances, all directing her thoughts toward the tenuous reality of her own existence. Laying her head back on the car seat, she was visited in this state of consciousness by an image of a long and dimly perceived passage which they were slowly traversing, a kind of tunnel with light at the end that both expanded and contracted. In one of these contractions a figure approached, or rather seemed to approach as they drew nearer. Its wings were translucent, but when they were near enough she saw that what hovered before them was not the angel which she had suspected but a hummingbird.

"It's the nicest thing that's happened to us in a long time," he had said, referring to the hummingbird nest they had discovered that May, directly above their front door in the branch of their blossoming crabapple tree. She had watched the mother bird morning and evening, putting out a feeder for her, and finally she had seen the two diminutive heads of the baby birds emerge above the edge of the nest, itself scarcely larger than a thimble. And then one rain-soaked morning he had awakened her at dawn to tell her that the birds were dead. He had gone out for the morning paper and found their tiny bodies, gray-feathered and hardly detectable, lying motionless on the front walk beneath a soggy and sagging nest. They had buried the dead birds in the back yard under a honeysuckle bush, and from some twigs and a piece of string she had fashioned a thumb-sized cross to mark the spot.

St. Petersburg, arid-looking even in its subtropical setting, proved a disappointment to her when they finally arrived: leveled and low-lying, its insubstantial buildings formed random cubes in the pastel light, all laced with a maze of wiring strung overhead and all set in seemingly endless blocks of asphalt and concrete which crowded out trees and grass. Nevertheless, she sensed his warming optimism. He had managed to obtain a street map of the Tampa Bay area when they stopped for gas that morning, and now that he had located Sixth Avenue, albeit at the wrong end of the city, his hope for a successful conclusion to their journey seemed rekindled.

"My guess is that the north end of this avenue is clustered with apartment buildings," he speculated, "and they're in one of them." Through five o'clock traffic they made their way north on the avenue to find that the first part of his guess, at least, was right. Not up to the task at hand, she wanted a motel and a shower first—they had stopped every night, but it seemed to her now that her clothes had been sticking to her for the entire trip. But he was unwilling to risk the time it would take to stop now, fearing they might somehow arrive too late, communicating a quiet anxiety to her in such a way that she went along without insisting. She felt her own heart accelerate as they turned off at the address they had and began to search for the apartment number—a false turn, as it happened, stumping them until his inquiry revealed that they were on the wrong side of Sixth Avenue.

"Even numbers should be on this side," he fretted, returning to the car. "We may have missed them in the meantime."

"We don't even know if they're still here," she thought to say, but she kept the thought to herself.

Exploring the other side of the avenue, where the two-storied complex subdivided into units that looked smaller and less expensive than their counterparts across the thoroughfare, they located, finally, the number they were looking for—an upstairs apartment next to the one at the near end of an oblong building, anonymous behind drawn curtains, possibly even vacant.

She felt her heart sink, but already he had climbed the stairs to the landing and begun to knock at the door, and just as he did so a third time she thought she might have seen the curtains move just a little.

"Nothing," he reported, coming down again. He decided to try to locate the manager's office, provided she would keep an eye on the place. She took a seat on the curb which commanded the approach from the parking lot, turning her head to watch him, with a twinge of misgiving, as he disappeared around the corner of the building.

She was searching her purse for an aspirin when she heard the muffled sound of a door closing behind and above her. Turning, she saw them at once, her son looking thinner than she remembered and looking worried so that it crossed her mind that maybe, God forbid, he had developed an ulcer, his face looking hurt, too, but relaxing just in the instant that she, having advanced on him, was flinging her arms around him and then feeling gratefully that he was hugging her, too, but conscious, even as he did so, that his wife had blurted "What are you doing here?" at her while she headed for the parking lot, so that she could not help wondering again what it was that they had ever done to her, to the wife who was sitting waiting for Loren now in the driver's seat of their car, to earn her spite.

There followed an exchange in which she heard him explaining without a hint of apology in his voice—it was his face, which seemed to struggle with mixed emotions, that betrayed him—that they had a meeting to attend, that they had determined, further, to have nothing to do with family for awhile, and when he pulled away and started to leave she thought of his father and began saying such things as "Wait, your father's here, too, and we've come all this way to see you," and "Weren't you even going to let us in?" and, remembering in her desperation, "Oh please wait, we have some peaches for you," and she went to look for his father then, glancing back once to see her son lingering and circling there and feeling the tears begin to well in her eyes as she did so. She wondered what could their meeting be that called them away, but whatever it was that separated them she could only dimly guess at.

Giving up her search for his father, she was returning to plead again with her son, but she caught herself, refusing to intrude on the scene before her, just as they both came into view. Their quest, she realized, had culminated in this desperate and doomed reunion of a few fleeting minutes, and in another this son, too, might be gone forever from their lives, and yet this final encounter redeemed in part their effort, for there at journey's end stood the father in his moment alone with the son, holding him close, telling this living one, she was sure, the things he had never been able to say to the one they had lost.

The Eighth World of Royden Taul

I

The concept of the Eight World, as far as I am aware, was the invention of my late colleague, Royden Taul, who expounded its virtues to our little group in impromptu and piecemeal fashion when we convened for our summer meetings in the garden-like suburbs of Chicago's west end. We were all older men well over the hill, save for young Matt Heyman, our leader's son, when Royden first showed up among us—our missing eighth, as it happened, recruited to fill our vacant Southern Plains territory.

Showed up, I say, when perhaps "materialized" is here the better choice, for strange to say I don't recall anyone taking notice of him until the meeting was formally begun. He may have slipped in at the last minute, of course, or he may have been the man I passed over who was surveying the hotel's well-kept grounds from our expansive bay window, with his back to the room, and whom I took to be a representative from one of our client publishers, the first on our agenda for the day.

Not that Royden was nondescript. Rawboned and ruddy, he seemed eminently noticeable, once introduced. His kindly blue eyes were set among crow's-feet, and his countenance in general, despite the sportive wisp of an auburn mustache, bore the weather-beaten marks of experience, perhaps not a little of it harsh and tainted with failure, so that from the outset there could be little doubt of his qualifications in years, at least, to join us aging bookmen. Such was our preferred designation, incidentally, for with college textbooks for our livelihood, we fancied ourselves the last remnants of an older and more gentlemanly profession. We were not, that is to say, your more recent brand of aggressive marketers who pressed their professors for book adoptions on the spot, against whom we pitted our more relaxed philosophy of "send them the book and let nature take its course," to recollect one of the more memorable tenets of "Old Max" Heyman. Instead, we conceived the art of the matter to be the judicious matching of the book with the class in which it could most likely be employed, following, of course, the diligent search for all such classes in question. And as Old Max had discerned, there remained the handful of unrepresented small presses "out there" who were willing to pay us commissions for just such work—work that we happened to love. Yet it was also work we needed, and a tendency among our clients to come and go put always an anxious edge to our good fortune.

But in just such work, and perhaps out of just such necessity, it should here be remarked that Royden was able to prove himself. Early on, I confess, he made a somewhat dubious start, for it must be allowed that his speech was at times afflicted with a slight but sad impediment, a hesitation of sorts which was most detectable at the very moments when he would speak most warmly to us. I suspect, moreover, that there were those present who never quite overcame their doubts about Royden from the day Old Max introduced him. True, he managed a passing smile, his eyes even twinkled, but he then sat the rest of the day out sunken in a meditative silence, and what was still more disturbing, with the corners of his mouth turned down in a possibly natural but nonetheless unseemly frown.

Yet such moods in him were rare, I came to understand, and I for one was ready to alter my first impression in the days that followed, days in which Royden acquitted himself by means of an obvious knowledge of books— particularly in the fields of history and politics, I noted approvingly. When, for example, a visiting editor introduced for us a text on the history of economic thought, Royden knew in a flash the book for us to "key" on ("keep an eye out for *The Worldly Philosophers*"), and before Old Max could turn him back to the book in our bewildered editor's hand, we had ourselves a thumb-nail sketch of Marxism, topped off with accolades for Norman Thomas, into whose campaign, we also learned, a youthful Royden had once thrown himself as a volunteer worker.

I found such devious trains of thought remarkable. Even so, I won't conceal that I found him most intriguing in those exchanges which took place beyond our conference table, where his quiet and sometimes puzzling pronouncements invariably fired my contemplations concerning his elusive Eighth World. Then too, there were also periods when he was neither the sphinx nor the prophet, but in fact quite like the rest of us. And this, I may venture, was a condition which the casual observer would have probably taken at best for a jaded complacency, a condition progressing to something soft and sluggish in us, I further suspect, for just when our prospects seemed darkest Old Max had announced a new publisher, an unanticipated benefactor who liked us so well that handsome and steady advances were thereafter forthcoming, and since the tenure of this guardian angel coincided with that of Royden in our group, the eventual result was no little speculation on the situation, as may be readily surmised.

But I myself am inclined to make no connection here, or else to admit that it's a story beyond my ken, and so to return to the one at hand, I judged that during such lapses in temperament as I was describing Royden Taul was simply resting or recuperating, and swallowing my disappointment, I thought to give the man his due.

II

"**B**ut what the hell is a smoking bench?" Hap Madrid, our man in Santa Barbara, was wanting to know—doubtless along with a number of us. His query came in response to Royden's proposal that we retire to the same after a day of meetings, his second or third with us, as I recall.

To which next day Royden responded in turn by steering us to a fitting example. Not two blocks from our hotel he'd located a rather rickety wooden picnic table with benches, as it developed, behind a small office building which sported a passing attempt at a colonial façade. Best of all, our backyard bench bordered upon a stretch of ground surprisingly rural, a bypassed and abandoned field now grown with briar and some stubby trees which cast for us dark silhouettes against the faintly luminous night sky. It was here that the four of us who were smokers took to retreating in the evenings, where we could languish in our veil of euphoric bliss, puffing at our leisure. On clear nights the stars were out for us, but even when not we had lights of the blinking kind to follow as the continuously arriving planes circled the city and sometimes veered out over the lake while waiting to descend upon O'Hare.

It was here, too, once of a Sunday evening—our weeklong conclaves invariably encompassed a weekend—that Royden was prodded beyond his usual speculations to a narrative with a personal touch, offered in further elaboration to his commentary on the "getaway." For it was true, that morning over breakfast Royden had chuckled derisively ("Was there anything more absurd?") while brandishing one of the several sleek supplements to the Sunday paper and pointing to its featured article, complete with color illustrations and the attendant ads of travel agencies, celebrating the weekend getaway.

"Ha!" Royden now responded. "Matter of fact I've been reminiscing some about that. Well now, boys, let me tell you the story of my first getaway—the first and only, as it happens."

We settled back expectantly, our little audience of three, having surveyed the night sky to our satisfaction.

"My ex-wife, Nita Sue, I like to think was behind it all. Always after me for us to 'Go somewhere, get out of Tulsa for a change,' she'd say, 'do something fun for once.' But I hadn't survived a war to go charging after excitement, and besides, at that time the college where I taught was paying me a miserable sum. I don't know where we could have gone if I had wanted to. In that respect we were like a lot of folks, which is still the case, I'll wager, in spite of what we see—or don't see, come to think of it. How about those poor bastards trapped in our inner cities, our cities' South Sides, the ones we don't see? Why, they're the ones that could use a getaway, and even for a weekend, don't you think?"

"But they've got theirs," Matt Heyman could not refrain from inserting. Royden, however, seemed ready for this, and he managed to stay on track, if barely.

"Ha! You see that, do you? Then how is ours any better, I ask you, even if ours we legalize—though maybe we damn well shouldn't, come to think. But no matter. All that's beside the point here, I suppose. Don't get me going on that.

"Anyway, that Nita Sue began to wear on me. Maybe a little change would do us good, I started to think. One fine morning in early May, a Saturday, I suggested we get in the car and indulge in a little trip.

"'But where are we going?' she wanted to know, surprised but delighted, if I wasn't mistaken.

"'Kenton, Oklahoma,' I told her. I'd been there once before, you see, one weekend in May when the sun was shining just as it was that morning, and I'd never quite forgotten what it was like. Don't miss it, boys, if ever you're out that way."

Here he paused, and young Matt seized his chance to inject an "I can't wait," eliciting a round of gentle mirth, which then subsided as Royden cleared his throat to resume.

"Well, I couldn't either, to tell the truth. We got past Enid and the traffic began to thin—I was keeping to the back roads, mind you, as I still do whenever I can. We drove through red clay landscapes, and I kept wondering if the place I had in mind was still the same. Out in the panhandle the land leveled out. We were in those parts called No Man's Land by then"—and here our Matt could not suppress an involuntary guffaw for punctuation.

"We got past the last of some foul-smelling feed lots, and rolled our windows down. The highway, narrow and deserted now, stretched out before us toward buttes and mesas—'the highest point in Oklahoma,' the road sign warned us. The land began to roll again. The grass had just turned green, the sky above was powder blue, and all around us meadowlarks were singing. Oh boys, I've never had a getaway like that one—and this is my first attempt, mind you.

"We topped a rise and there it was, the town of Kenton, just as I remembered it. It hadn't changed. It sat out there on the western end of Oklahoma just as it always had. I slowed to a snail's pace, and my heart was singing like the meadowlarks.

"There was the general store—two storied, wood-framed, a couple of gas pumps out front—for a center of interest. A place where four or five cars such as ours might stop in the course of an ordinary day, I'd guess, and every day was probably ordinary. Not enough, you say, but maybe just as it should be—maybe just what the proprietor wanted. Not much else, to be sure. A few scattered houses, one of them home to a flock of barn swallows now, from the looks of things.

"I'd had in mind a dinner for two at that general store, but first I had to stop and bask for awhile in the peace and warmth. I eased over into the weeds and grasses of the shoulder and cut the motor. There was the sweet smell of the grasslands on the breeze, and between the bursts of birdsong it was so quiet we could hear the grasshoppers jumping.

"I seemed to feel my soul unclenching. It was a bright mid-day in the middle of spring and the world seemed bright with promise. I was certain I had discovered the secret of the getaway: you find some out-of-the-way place such as this that the rest of the world has forsaken. Let them have the rest of it, I was thinking, and I was just on the verge of expressing my sentiments—'Why, this is heaven,' I started to sigh out loud—when Nita Sue beat me to the punch.

"Why, this is horrible," I heard her gasp, and I knew right then that she was one of them, and this the beginning of the end for us.

"And so the spell was broken—when I'd had plans to push on even further, to the llano country of New Mexico, land of abandoned homesteads, desolate and wonderful. Instead, we spent the night in the town of Guymon, metropolis of the Oklahoma panhandle, and drove home the next morning, Nita Sue in an embittered silence, which I suppose she had a right to.

"As for me, in spite of my paltry earnings, I couldn't wait to get back to work again—back to my calling, you might even have said of me, in those days. In those days, boys, I fancied myself a budding young historian, and what I wanted most in the world, don't you see, was not so much to get away from anything as to get more deeply into what I was doing. Ha! There's the crux of it all."

With this summation his voice trailed off in a somber way, infecting us with similar spirits, for this time no mirth escaped our lips. On the contrary, a contemplative mood prevailed. Then Royden Taul extinguished his cigarillo, grinding it on the surface of the old wooden table we'd gathered around. In the darkness I had the feeling he was gazing at us sternly. Then he spoke, his voice quiet and level.

"In the Eighth World, boys, there are no getaways."

III

Royden Taul was born in Oklahoma, the descendant of farmers, and as may become apparent, raised within at the least some vestigial sphere of the Bible Belt—a field of force identified by Mencken, as I recall, whose work Royden happened to admire.

"Like Mickey Mantle and Roy Harris," I heard him counter once when cited for being an "Okie" in the hotel lounge, where a group of us were being sociable at happy hour. There followed a moment of failed recollection on the part of Barry Rooney, our Northeast rep from Boston, who had made the accusation.

"Who the hell is Roy Harris?" He deliberated aloud. Then, "You mean the boxer? But wasn't he from someplace in Texas?"

Taking his cue, Royden proceeded to enlighten us about the American composer, concluding with an appreciation of his "great third symphony," a work of "quiet pastoral harmonies," as he described it, a work that "gathered its strength and power without a trace of bombast."

"How come we never hear it?" came the inquiry in the midst of our mulling this over, as if to justify our ignorance.

Royden Taul could not but smile.

"In the Eighth World," he replied, "it will live forever."

"The Eighth World," Matt Heyman chuckled the next morning at breakfast in the hotel coffee shop. "What happens to the Fifth and Sixth, or the Seventh?"

Royden arrested his spoon above his oatmeal.

"It takes an eighth," was his thoughtful reply.

"I see," his inquisitor relented, apparently not wishing to pursue the matter further, although I doubted that any of us "saw," as he put it with characteristic jocosity, or grasped the full intent of Royden's suggestive words.

I came to realize that such cryptic responses as Royden had uttered were often the source of mild amusement for some of my colleagues, provoking them to nothing more than a tolerant smile. Yet for me his words had the effect of riddles, providing me always with food for thought, and food for which I apparently hungered, so charged was my imagination. I deemed myself fortunate whenever I could get him going while there were just the two of us, without the distraction of those inclined to take him less seriously.

When able to do so, I steered him toward the homeless and the disappearing middle class, those aberrations of a system which should have been, or so at least it seemed to me, the increasing concern of us all. And they were, I am sure, allotted a high priority among his seemingly vagrant imaginings, for upon his arrival at such topics as these he might share his insights as if from a kind of trance.

"In the Eighth World," he told me once at the end of a day as we stretched our legs on the sidewalks, "you will find no knowledge of poverty. Oh, poverty,

36

yes, by our standards," he added, seeing me wonder. "But remember, Charlie, the words of Our Lord, which will at last be heeded there."

I was in the midst of inquiring, "'Be not anxious'... do you mean?" when he gave me still more to ponder.

"The same with wealth," he added again. "There will be no knowledge of wealth."

IV

Although bred of farmers, Royden Taul had endeavored to earn his living as a teacher, as suggested in his "getaway" story, but I also learned that, as the "budding young historian" alluded to in that same narrative, he had once aspired to make his reputation in the world as a writer. And though it was now apparent that any such aspirations had been subsequently modified, he still took up his pen on occasion if only to "clarify his own thinking," as he explained it, about those issues which most concerned him. In the beginning, he had paid particular attention to the poor, as evidenced by his first published work, grown out of a master's thesis in history composed when he was still a young man, detailing the hardships of Oklahoma homesteaders. From there he turned his attention to a well documented account of the widespread exploitation in the copper mines of Arizona, which in selected circles earned for him, I gathered, a brief notoriety.

It was following this success that he conceived and began his most ambitious undertaking, tentatively titled *The Lackey System in America*, he once divulged while reminiscing with that sporadic but by then familiar twinkle in his eye. And I here recall the grandness of that title—not overlooking, as I seem to sense, a simultaneous homage to some absurdity within it—if only to show what must have been the mounting fervor of his thinking. Before he was well into it, however, something happened to him, some interruption, I was led to assume. Returning to it, he'd set the work aside with a realization of his limitations, which from the beginning the scope of the project had deemed inevitable. He never took it up again.

During the years I called myself his colleague his efforts were confined to relatively brief essays, often with rather playful or at least unorthodox titles, which he occasionally placed in those small-circulation journals still retaining "a social conscience," as he required of them. Of such substance, to recall the first which comes to mind, was his "Aspects of the Doppus Effect," a piece exploring some consequences of a trend he had watched and deplored in higher education, a trend toward the contemporary and the "falsely relevant," as he defined it, at the expense of history and the genuine.

In these lesser accomplishments the perception seemed keen enough, the

37

flashes of imagination brilliant enough, to make me wonder why he had elected to confine his talent, for so it seemed to me. And when he had abandoned, in who can fathom what depths of despair, that envisioned but never completed magnum opus, *The Lackey System in America*, who can guess what may have been forever lost to the world—save perhaps to the Eighth World, come to think, where, according to Royden Taul, nothing of worth was ever wholly lost.

V

Even though Royden Taul had somewhere curtailed his aspirations as a writer, during his third summer with us he nevertheless revealed to me that he was about to involve himself in "a work of the imagination"—a novel, maybe, although more likely, he quickly emended, something less ambitious, perhaps some Mencken-like polemic. There were just the two of us present at our bench that evening, a circumstance that doubtless encouraged his disclosures. I had been a little late arriving, and coming upon Royden seated in a wistful solitude, consoled no doubt with musings on his private World, I perceived all of a sudden how friendless and alone he was in this one, and I could not suppress a pang of feeling for the man.

The "work," as Royden began to dwell upon it, had germinated from his preoccupation with the theme of crime in our time, a theme he felt the media had possibly exaggerated. Thus, in what seemed to me a rather extreme interpretation of the matter, we were in devious ways made wary of a criminal element which multiplied in our streets while "ordinary upright citizens" quailed in alarm, their very confidence in one another taxed to the limit, so that Royden envisioned a world in which the former at last tipped the scales against the latter. The outcome, he reasoned, could only be a nation entangled in its prisons, the latest census revealing that those within this dubious system now surpassed, if only by a head or two, those supposedly without—"supposedly," I was made to see, because the discerning individual could appreciate at once the difficulty in determining, under those evolving circumstances, just who were the incarcerated, and who were not.

"Consider, Charlie, the possibilities," he inveighed, while I blinked against the nightmare he had sketched. "Do I invoke a kind of Saturnalian switch in which your 'ordinary citizens,' if any be, scramble for the security of the prison walls, and turn the inmates out? Bringing with them, of course, all their worldly goods that they can muster, yet even so, for safety's sake willing to jettison much—the wealthier classes, in particular, abandoning in the process large holdings in real estate." Here he paused, displayed that twinkle in his eye, and softly added an irrepressible aside: "All of this has struck me as a kind of dutiful acquiescence, if only under duress, to Our Lord's advice to the rich young man."

I had once again to marvel at the man and his "possibilities," as he called his wild inventions—and yet they were not too far-fetched, either, to arrest my willing attention.

"And once in motion," he resumed, "who's to say where the process stops? Screening themselves, as well they might, would not a certain criminality begin to manifest itself within the ranks of those who were now walled in—just as it did while they were at large and without? Would not the chief deterrent to these transgressors, the traitors within the walls, so to speak, now be the feeble threat of eviction, expulsion from prison—the very reversal of former sentencing, mind you, before the world turned topsy-turvy?

"Eventually I'd be obliged to place the dwindling party of the 'good guys' holed up in island fortresses—a revamped Alcatraz, let's say—with equally dwindling stores of necessities, and no more National Guard to call upon. And what of those without, that ever widening plurality of humankind? Should we portray one long continuous frenzy of looting—a merger, say, of L.A. riots with New York City brownouts?

"Ha! The possibilities!" He rummaged even further in his bag of tricks. "Do gangs, however painfully, evolve to armies, and on to rudimentary governments in the process? Do laws and even medicine achieve new pinnacles of enlightenment?"

We stared at one another, and I could sense his mind still working at some last cause, a thing more grave than he had so far touched upon.

"Consider also this. Imagine, at last, this whole Industrial Revolution, as we call it, grinding to a halt, and all our damned and ruinous traffic finally balked. Does earth seize the moment to heal itself, and into the bargain heal humanity too? It's an ill wind if it doesn't, for this could be the stuff our Eighth World waits upon."

VI

But before proceeding, and in part in preparation for what follows, I feel the need to remark again on the impediment of speech previously alluded to, and on the attendant matter of the mouth, which on occasion found its equilibrium in a natural frown, as already stated. Since scant detail of either trait has thus far appeared for inspection, I might here attempt to elaborate, and while not implying that Royden was free from contradiction, I might attempt in the process to explain what must appear by now a contrary phenomenon—that robust "Ha!" of Royden's, suggesting a man well informed as to where he meant to proceed with his discourse.

To begin with the disobedient mouth, it seemed the single blemish in a countenance which otherwise bespoke the best goodwill, at unguarded moments betraying this intended demeanor by exposing some deeper complication, for as if some ugliness coiled within sought release there, the mouth on these occasions slumped downward in a frown of universal disapproval, disconsolate and dour. "Disobedient," I've impugned it, for often Royden himself was not unconscious of the tendency, and, at least in public, strove mightily to control it. Rousing himself from one of his abstract ruminations—which is to say from his natural inclination—he was himself dismayed, I believe, to discover he was frowning, and on the spot would summon certain alterations he took to be more becoming. Be it said that these self-conscious wrestlings took place with few exceptions within the closed chamber of our conference room, for outside of it some tension seemed to relax in him. Within, however, the end result was not unpredictable: a man who never really found himself at ease, his mouth, a thing divorced from the rest of him, so forced and malleable as to beget him nothing better than a continuity of contrived expressions, none of which seemed genuine.

Then too, the disease was communicable. Even good-natured Old Max, glancing sidewise at his new recruit to find him in the possession of his demon, might withdraw from us for a while his characteristic smile of approval. Aware of this effect, Royden was rendered the more uneasy with himself. The same, perhaps, as some rough workman, finding himself removed to a nicely furnished parlor room and seated amidst polite conversation, might belabor the conduct of his hands, so Royden's constant worry was what to do with is mouth.

As to that related difficulty pertaining to the mouth's emanations, this eccentricity, too, was largely confined to the meeting room, where most of us were prepared to bear with him. When at his best, he never failed to enlighten us. At worst, however, our patience gave way to embarrassment as his brash and self-confident "Ha's," born of other circumstances, reversed themselves and came out a trio of tremulous "Ah's"—and this, as often as not, in the midst of a sentence which seemed otherwise well conceived. Launched upon a sentence of promising import, he might seem suddenly confronted with a surfeit of alternatives. Thus the hesitations—the outright haltings at times—as Royden fumbled to revise himself at midstream, scuttling himself in the end with that sputtering "Ah, ah, ah." Such times as these, we mostly turned away from him.

And yet, as already hinted, despite these tribulations there remained an area where Royden seemed exempt from all impairment, a single topic upon which the corners of his mouth held upward of their own volition and his speech flowed unimpeded—or better, with confidence and almost eagerly. For on the subject of the Eighth World, he never faltered.

VII

The four of us were this time gathered to indulge our habit when the serenity of the summer evening was momentarily perturbed by the siren of a passing police car, and Royden Taul made use of the interruption to volunteer that he had been reading and reflecting much upon the literature of criminological theory. It being the evening which succeeded his vision of a world enmeshed in epidemic crime, I braced myself for a possible sequel to those wild speculations, but to Hap Madrid and young Matt Heyman the proposal which Royden put forth was little more than a jest. Royden, I am sure, was neither surprised nor offended by this, and if I here record the incident it is primarily in order to relate what passed between the two of us later.

Royden, it seemed, had been struck by the recurrent references in his reading to a probable root cause for the phenomenon of crime, which was that the capacity for empathy on the part of the perpetrator was often defective— in some cases, indeed, totally absent. Becoming much engrossed with the implications of this theory, he had reached the conclusion that this was surely an explanation which "works both ways," as he expressed it.

"Without empathy, boys, I think I may have presumed to judge the want of the same in some other," he confessed. "I take it the words of Our Lord touched on the subject when He asked who would cast the first stone."

Thus was he warming to his proposition for us, the rudiments of which, in short, amounted to this: that if some lack of empathy, or the proper capacity to place oneself in the shoes of another, were the root culprit in our problem of crime, shouldn't we "ordinary citizens" be willing to exercise ourselves in the same sentiment? And how better to empathize with the part of the criminal, he pursued, than to involve ourselves in a crime? Preferably, in order to explore the full effects on the psyche, in a premeditated crime, or better yet, in a "series of crimes," though he seemed willing to stop short of giving ourselves over to a life of crime.

"Jesus," Matt Heyman exhaled. "For a minute there I thought it was going to be 'commit the crime of your choice.' What'll it be for us, guys, abduction and rape?"

With just such merriment was Royden's proposal dissipated upon the air of the once again benign evening, but perhaps I alone, after the conversation had drifted to less remarkable topics, continued to mull the matter over, there having been just enough edge to Royden's voice to encourage me to do so.

"Seriously," I approached him later that night, back at the hotel lounge where I'd talked him into a nightcap. "I'm curious. Just what kind of crime did you have in mind?"

He smiled but hesitated, as if unwilling to return to the subject his colleagues had brushed aside with such lightheartedness.

"I had in mind some crime of property."

I waited. "Nothing more specific?" I coaxed.

He turned on me then a look of sudden mischievousness, boyish but quickened with irony.

"I was considering a pick-pocketing campaign in broad daylight, or perhaps an elaborately planned burglary in the dead of night."

He blinked, still ruminating, and I watched his mouth begin to writhe. I half expected that next would come the stammer, but instead his expression gave way to something more hardened, some darker ambivalence the like of which I had never faced in him before, and I felt the night, no longer benign, begin to invade my heart.

"But you know," he at last added slowly, "I've been thinking, Charlie. Abduction and rape is not at all a bad idea."

"But the Eighth World," I pleaded. "I had pictured it free of crime and violence. Surely you don't mean to say...do its people engage in crime?"

He held me steadfastly in that hardened gaze he had assumed, triumphant, with just a tremor of amusement for my discomfort.

"Doesn't everybody?" he asked me evenly.

VIII

At the start of Royden's fourth year with us we missed him at the summer meeting, where we were informed he had suffered a stroke of some sort.

"Hopefully nothing too serious," Max Heyman sought to reassure us. "Apparently it took his doctor to tell him about it. He didn't know he'd had it."

It was known, however, that Royden was late to hit the road that fall, and I doubt that he covered his territory to the extent prescribed and expected by Old Max, whose heart was too soft, nonetheless, to dismiss him.

When we beheld him in person again the following summer, there was a perceptible limp in his left leg, and on the same side of his body he now wore a hearing aid. Attentive in our sessions, he was not so restless as we remembered him, more subdued, and less given to the tangents we had come to expect of him. When he did speak, his voice seemed hoarse. Even at the smoking bench, a custom we had maintained in his absence, he now seemed content to listen. I hungered for further enlightenment about that enigmatic World which only he could impart, it now being two years since he had thus instructed us, but I found myself reluctant to disturb his peace. Toward the end of our week together, however, a chance remark induced a regression to something of his old withdrawal, at least for an afternoon.

It was Barry Rooney, if memory serves me, who that afternoon at the conference table evoked the term "brainwashing," the phrase which sounded the alarm to Royden. As though compelled to account for every face present, he shot furtive glances around the table, but then his gaze turned inward, his mouth collapsed, and his whole being slumped into a stolid pout, lost to us for the remainder of the day.

It was a concept which belonged to the fifties, of course, and that a decade, as rumor had it, in which Royden Taul had done some time in a North Korean prison camp. It was a rumor to which I, for one, gave credence, for I fancied that here was a missing piece to the unfinished puzzle we had of the man. I thought of torture, deprivation and indoctrination, but whether or not any of this was a part of Royden's experience we would never know, for it was plain that on the matter his lips were sealed.

On the final day of our meeting, however, it was Royden himself who returned to the concept, though in my presence only, and somewhat uncertainly at that. With the boon of an afternoon off, three of us had passed it at the nearby Morton Arboretum, and having strolled the acres of pastoral beauty to be experienced there, we were confronted on our return with its man-made counterpart: six lanes of swiftly flowing rush-hour traffic—that entity so abhorred by Royden—separating us from our hotel.

What I recall of the ensuing incident seems dreamlike, and yet it could only be a dream that's shared by two of us, for there's a witness to the scene. I have this vision of the three of us—Royden, Matt Heyman and me—considering our chances at fording that terrible torrent at mid-block, the nearest intersection being a good half-mile out of our way. The curbing and the asphalt seem fresh and new, but this thoroughfare, like many another, has not been planned with pedestrians in mind, even though beyond the far curb the urban sprawl has bypassed a field of weeds, some of them tall and gone to flower.

We hesitate, and then before we know it our Matt has waded into the current, bobbing and darting as the waters seem to whimsically part for him, and while we look on with mingled disapproval and relief, in a final agile dash he gains the farther shore.

"Oh to be young and daring," I remark to Royden, as the object of our observation tosses us, from across that intimidating river, a dismissive wave and a slightly superior smile.

"See you geezers later," he boasts, and he leaves us to fend for ourselves.

"Talk about brain-washed," I hear Royden complain. I glance again at Matt departing, but I'm soon aware that his reference is to something more immediate. He's glowering at the passing drivers behind their windshields, as if, like a wolf, he's about to single one of them out.

"Ha! Sheep!" he growls, eyes suddenly bright, then ponders aloud, his voice gone hoarse—alluding to "Our Lord" again, if I'm not mistaken, and something about a "thief in the night."

Mumbling thus, he breaks off and fixes his gaze straight before him, sticks up a hand like a traffic cop, and to my great consternation, goes limping deliberately into the roiling waters. Brakes screech, horns blare, and from somewhere back in the ranks a man with his window down is yelling and cursing. I turn away, catching a glimpse as I do of Matt down the far sidewalk, who's stopped and turned to stare. I'm anticipating the thud of steel impacting flesh and bone, signaling the abrupt cessation of Royden's devil-may-care demonstration, and I can't bear to watch.

Yet somehow it never happens. No, I can't say for sure that I've seen him safe on the opposite shore, but no one is down in the street, and the traffic has closed over the charmed but foolhardy path he was cutting, resuming its usual pace. Needless to say, I myself take the long way around, making use of the distant intersection with its traffic signal and attaining at length our hotel, where Matt Heyman, while admitting that he too lost sight of Royden in the midst of his heroics, corroborates that I haven't been dreaming.

"Missing person," he laughs it off. "Call the police."

But I spend the better part of my evening reflecting. Still troubled by the oblivion to wealth and poverty which Royden attributed to Eighth World inhabitants, I wonder whether this same attitude cannot be summoned against traffic—or indeed, against whatever terrors they care to invoke it. And whether oblivion is not, after all, a means of seeing, and the one true antidote to our world as it is.

IX

The next morning I was left to assume that Royden had taken an early cab to the airport, for I discovered that he had, indeed, checked out, reassuring me at least of his survival. Sensing the end of something, nevertheless, I supposed that there was no denying that the man was part magician, for having "materialized" for us in the beginning and then evaded a stroke, hadn't he now proceeded to his disappearing act, perhaps the ultimate "getaway," or even the abduction he had found so appealing, with himself the willing victim, whisked away to his "No Man's Land," a wayward son brought home to a World whose bounds would remain forever just beyond our laymen's comprehension.

I sensed the end of something, yes, but I was soon to find that fate had reserved for me a final interview with Royden. I like to think it took place because out of all our little group, which within the year would begin to crumble and fail, I was his most earnest disciple, and though I cannot speak for

Royden, I could not at the time foresee that within the same year a second and fatal stroke was lying in wait for him.

As was my habit, I arrived at O'Hare in time to check my bags an hour before my flight. I was making my way toward my gate when who should I stumble upon, in one of the uncountable waiting areas that lined that great terminal's multiple corridors, but our "missing person" of the day before. He sat a little apart from his fellow travelers, slumped in his rumpled topcoat, dejected because his flight had been delayed. I had intended to read, but seeing him waiting there alone in the crowd I experienced a wave of vague regret, and I suggested we kill some time with one for the road. He preferred instead to walk "outside in the sun"—he hated the air conditioning, which had given him a chill.

"Besides," it occurred to him, "I could use the exercise."

And so outside on the sidewalk, in humid air and hazy sunlight, we two "geezers" were able to stretch our legs together one last time.

"The work," I reminded, breaking our silence when we had walked awhile. "That germinating 'polemic' you spoke of once—on the topic of crime, you may remember. May I read it when it's ready?"

"Ha, that," he allowed. "No you may never, that one. Lost interest, I suppose." Another empty boast, I found myself thinking, but then I heard him utter my thoughts aloud.

"Or better, I suppose, an empty boast. I should have done so when I could have," he added. Shamed, I remembered that this was a man who had suffered much, and thought to ease him toward that subject dear to his heart, recalling for him the riddle he had once employed in our hotel coffee shop.

"It takes an eighth," I reflected out loud. "Did you mean," I ventured, "an eighth of human nature?"

"Half again of half of us is twice what we have, as I calculate."

"Oh, then," I offered, thinking I grasped his intention. "It takes an eighth of the population...to bring it about?"

Stunned, he stopped us both in our tracks, and eyed me squarely. "To bring it about?" he almost whispered.

I stared at him in return. Was this the magician's final illusion, I wondered, held in reserve among his repertoire for this climactic act? But no, the surprise and disappointment in his voice had been too real for that, and confronted with the mute entreaty of the face my query had brought to bear on me, I saw I had obviously wronged the man. More likely, it was just that now and the future were one and the same for him, and, never intended for deception, that last, hoarsely intoned and unforgettable "To bring it about?" was to prove for me an unintended revelation—a parting blessing, if you will, in what was to be, our final encounter.

For at last I began to understand. The Eighth World, I realized, was not to be "brought about," as if lurking unborn. If it existed at all, its existence was here and now. And it did exist, I gradually came to believe, if only one knew where and how to look for it. Since when the longer I live—the older I grow and the more alone—I have for my increasing consolation the World as bequeathed by Royden Taul, the more of which I begin to see.

Llano Country

Just south and west of Kenton, Oklahoma, out on the Llano Estacado on the vast east side of New Mexico, someone has been laying out a parking lot. It's adjacent to what appears to be a ghost town, the name of which is preserved in the seven faded but still legible letters on the weatherbeaten face of a water tower, leaning but still standing on the far edge of town: "PERDIDO," they seem to whisper, though few, if any, pass this way to heed them. It's uncharted miles to the whine of the nearest interstate, and surely the addition of the parking lot does not forebode yet another tourist trap—unless, of course, some gross miscalculation has occurred.

Now at the height of summer the asphalt is still fresh in the parking lot, releasing its sweet pungency beneath the morning sun, but ragged already at the edges where hollyhocks and black-eyed Susans have begun to intrude. The bank and the general store, the hotel with its saloon, the jail with the sheriff's office are all lined up and ready, just as you'd expect to see them, as well as a leftover building with a trace of gilt lettering high on its false façade, a building of indeterminate function. The parking lot is empty.

Across the street there's an opera house and a telegraph office, and wandering about for a larger perspective you can see a church and a schoolhouse in fresh white paint, the livery stable and the blacksmith's shop, and of course, on another back street, the inevitable House of Joy—all things you'd expect and want to see there, not to mention the crumbling mill, abandoned when the creek went dry.

Later, in the hotel dining room, to judge from the just audible clinking of china and crystal, someone is dining alone. Out on the Llano the white-rumped antelope pause in their grazing to listen, curious. The jubilance of the meadowlarks has subsided along with the morning, and in the heat of the early afternoon the only other sound is the occasional "click" of a grasshopper jumping.

Still later, while the last of the setting sun is aflame in the upstairs windows, someone is strolling at his leisure. His boots thump out a slow-paced rhythm on the board sidewalk, a sound that ceases while he pauses, rolls himself a smoke, leans on an antique hitching post, and then begins to inhale as he studies for a moment the just emerging evening star. In the gathering darkness he's hard to follow, but it's certain that like a watchman on his beat he's taking a turn about the town. There's the ring of metal striking metal in the vicinity of the blacksmith's shop, a sudden, solitary blow. A little later, the prevailing quiet is disturbed again by just the faintest chuckle near the House of Joy. Strangely, though, when seen again someone is standing as if in meditation before the building of indeterminate function, which stares back vacant-eyed, its windows catching the feeble light of the streetlamp in front of the opera house. He may be mistaken, but he thinks he can just make out that the last gilt letter on the false façade was once an "x", but then again, he considers, it could be a "v" or even a "y" with its tail now missing, which seems more likely to him. He's distracted at last by an almost electrical beeping from the sky above the telegraph office—the cry of a nighthawk passing.

And so the sunlit days and the star-bright nights tumble on, the nights gaining ground on the days as the season changes. The parking lot remains empty. For more than a month no one has been seen or heard. Only the moon is waxing, and out on the Llano the yipping bark of the coyotes erupts into mournful howling—just as you've come to expect of them. The meadowlarks have flown.

Deep into autumn, if such a thing were possible the parking lot looks even emptier—perhaps because the hollyhocks are withered, the black-eyed Susans blasted. Curious, the white-rumped antelope drift in to the edge of it, lifting their heads to stare. Curiously, too, the building of indeterminate function looms taller than before, or, more likely, it's simply that everything else seems shrunken and shriveled with aging.

And as if such a thing were possible, as if at some point in the day without our awareness, the silence has assumed a voice. Somewhere, someone is weeping. Yes, it is there, somehow, this human weeping—it is what we are hearing now. Impossible to say whether it's a woman or a man, or where, exactly, the sound can be coming from: a room upstairs in the hotel, the vicinity of the crumbled mill, the graveyard behind the church—or perhaps from the vacant-eyed building that looms taller than ever, almost indeterminable now? Wait: is it one, or is it a hundred we hear? Impossible to say, except that it's the town itself that seems to be shuddering, sobbing almost in silence—surely it is all like nothing we ever expected to witness or hear. Then at last as the sun goes down the speechless windows assume their brief but familiar glow.

Out on the Llano a storm is picking up. It is late and turning cold, and into the town the wind comes whistling and moaning, driving before it a couple of tumbleweeds. The dust's too thick to see him, with darkness gathering, but up and down and to and fro someone has been limping, someone who seems to be leaving now. Of course, we could be mistaken, but listen: perhaps you can just make out, between the wind's gasps, the silvery tinkling of his spurs.

Fool's Paradise

"**D**on't laugh, gentlemen. I could tell you a story about a geezer."

The three of us turned toward the shadow-fallen face of our companion. From our vantage point of the foothill terrace of the inn, we had been aimlessly surveying the desert city, unreal and lovely with its lights aglow in the twilight sky. Far up the valley to the north, toward the Sangre de Cristo Range, we'd watched a lordly tower of cumulonimbus billowing in the last light of the summer day.

"He was wearing one of those green plastic visors, the kind you see sometimes on card players and pool hall hustlers. His pants were too short—high water pants, I guess you'd call them—and you could see where his dirty white socks were fallen and bunched around the anklebone. I'll never forget him, and I'm sure Bye never would have either."

Norman Flinders seldom spoke so much at once, but when he did we were compelled to listen. He had a measured way of softening and yet intensifying his voice, signaling one of those infrequent but morally replete narratives he deemed worthy of the serious attention of "gentlemen," as he liked to address us on such occasions. He had his lighter side too, of course, but even this could seem deceptively serious at times.

Big Frank McFall chortled. "High water pants," he repeated, grinning like a man who had just recognized an old friend. "I haven't heard that one in a coon's age." His drawl betrayed the Texan that he was. A good, big-hearted one at that, as well as an imposing hulk of a man, his trusted temperament had earned for him the affectionate epithet with which he was customarily designated—an epithet, be it added, which had inspired Flinders on some forgotten occasion to announce that he himself was "just a middle-sized Norman," and so christen himself a redundant "Medium Norm." So too from Flinders had our Big Frank won the esteemed but still ironic appraisal of "The West Texas Humanist," having once abandoned the faculty of a small church college in Abilene because, as only he could put such things, he'd gotten "tired of being moral." Still, for as long as we'd known him he'd been back in harness, like John Robinson Fairchild, his doubles partner of the morning, professing at the state university. Flinders and I were academic exiles, merely, confirmed travelers both, but annually at the appointed weekend for nearly a decade now the four of us had found ourselves thus situated at the New Paradise Inn, where we splurged for a round of tennis and the pleasures of fellowship in plush surroundings—though I often sensed the place inspired uneasiness in Flinders, some obscure nerve of his being agitated by the luxury of it. We were four old duffers in our sixties now, and very conscious of it—reason enough, I suppose, for Big Frank's way of making light of it. As I recall it was his allusion to "those poor geezers" in the county hospital—a massive, well lit structure that figured prominently against the city's darkening skyline—that touched off the peculiarly restrained but charged voice of our narrator.

"Of course you fellows never knew 'Bye' Johnson," he was saying. "In those days, gentlemen, when I was a kid over in Tucson, I was considered very promising at this game." He indicated one of the rackets we'd discarded on the table next to us. "And Bye wasn't at all bad himself, as well as being lucky. He got his nickname drawing byes at all the tournaments, free passes. In a lean year he made it to the finals of the State Open with only one win. A bye, two defaults, and a marathon win over a guy who'd made it to the semis in more or less the same way. He was the luckiest guy around—up to a point, anyway.

"And he was a handsome devil, too. One of those tall, soft-spoken guys with straight black hair that you see a lot in Texas—Big Frank, you know the type. I once saw him walk right up to a good-looking girl while she was playing a tournament match on an adjacent court. 'Pardon me, Miss. What is your name?' he asked, and before you knew it he'd charmed her into playing mixed doubles with him, just for starters. He was four years my senior and, needless to say, gentlemen, my idol.

"I suppose, though, there are a couple of things I should add about him. I never understood it at the time—still don't, altogether—but he wasn't a popular kind of guy. For one thing, he didn't play the kind of game that captured the imagination of most people. No, he was a heady kind of player. He relied on groundstrokes and a great lob which he knew when to use. Then too there was a lot of talk around that you'd better not play him without an umpire, that he'd call them on you. That reputation, I thought, was unfounded and undeserved, but it persisted. And it wasn't just the men. Girls usually didn't like him either, at least not after they had known him for awhile, I noticed. He'd go with a good-looker for awhile, and then you'd see her at some tournament rooting for his opponent—along with almost everybody else. That was the case with this one sun-browned doll on the women's team at U. of A. Her name was Donna Martel and she was everybody's dream. Jesus, what a body. She'd play in the tournaments down in Tucson and none of the men could concentrate. When Bye started taking up with her my idolatry was complete, I can tell you. Yet she was just like the others. It didn't last long, and when I saw her at the State Open that spring, pulling against Bye, it left me somewhat hurt and puzzled. I think these things hurt Bye sometimes, too, even if he was a cocky kind of guy on the surface. I'd catch him staring rather sadly in Donna Martel's direction after the thing was over with. I often saw him in a pensive mood when he thought no one was looking.

"Anyway, we were both what were called promising young players and we'd talked a little about taking off together some summer and 'playing the circuit,' as the phrase went. Bye had already done it a year or two, but that was still my dream. And it wasn't just the tournaments, you understand. There was also the travel. Getting off on our own. A new town every week, and of course, girls."

"Hot damn!" Big Frank interjected. "Now you're talkin'."

"You've got the picture," Flinders assured. "Two kids off on a lark in the early 'fifties. Those were the days." He paused while Big Frank lit a cigar, of sorts—cigarillos, he called the things—the rest of us having declined the ones he'd proffered.

"Would that I had never outlived those days. In one sense, though, I suppose I haven't. I still have a thing about traveling—as you fellows may know, and understand, even." He paused again, smiled, and sought me out. "Charlie here, for instance, Charlie out there on that llano."

He alluded, we knew, to the slight little piece I'd read to them the previous night upon our arrival—a kind of postscript to a longer work I'd probably never try on them, though it once drew a few kind words from my late wife.

"Amen to that," I allowed. Below us, on a second neatly gardened terrace, a young couple seated at poolside with their backs toward us were silhouetted by the subsurface lights. At odd intervals the woman's laughter drifted up to us, providing the only commentary to Flinders' voice, which once again took up the narrative that seemed to claim all his concentration.

"Yes, road maps were a source of continual fascination for me. Spread one out before me and I could spend the day studying it, and the next day go through it all again. And yes, gentlemen, I could still do it. I've never gotten over it. You could set the house on fire and charm me into a studied immobility with a road map. To me it's like that cigar there to Big Frank. Or worse, much worse, I'm sure. Like booze to those who can't do without it. So when you talk about county hospitals, aluminum walkers and 'the geezer shelter,' gentlemen, you depress me profoundly. Because when that day comes, you see, it's over for me. Without the prospect of the road I'm as good as dead. It's been that way since the summer I was seventeen, and I've never gotten over it.

"The summer I was seventeen. That's the summer we took off together, Bye Johnson and I. It was to be a kind of modified circuit—a couple of 'tuners,' as Bye called them, and then the big one for us, the Heart of America in Kansas

City. We were two promising young men with the world before us, and I was in a heaven of anticipation.

"We took off from Tucson for Las Vegas, the site of our first tuner, in Bye's black '50 Oldsmobile. He'd acquired it at a bargain price from some widow who had hardly used it, and it went like a rocket, or so it seemed to me. He had it up to eighty a time or two as we crossed the desert.

"Well, as you fellows know by now, the best of prospects have a way of turning on you, and we weren't in Vegas long before it started to happen. Oh sure, there was a convertible for awhile, even a girl, a most remarkable one, though I only saw her once at that time. Still, tennis was my first love in those days, but there wasn't any tournament in town, and somehow we never even got around to checking out the courts.

"We slept on the floor in the apartment of a fellow named Chick Hardin. I was fast learning that Bye didn't believe in spending good money when it wasn't necessary—en route to Vegas he'd stopped at a little grocery, bought cookies and milk and called it dinner. Hardin had been his doubles partner one year at the U. of A., but he was dropped from the team—and the school—with a record of. cheating on exams. He had wavy blond hair, the build of Adonis, and a new Ford convertible. Our first night there he showed us the town in it. It was all new to me, and the place seemed fairly aflame. We toured up and down the Strip, his radio filling the night with music by people like the Four Freshmen. Those were the days.

"Our second night he lined Bye up with this dream of a showgirl named Laurel—I know because I went by her place in the convertible with Bye one evening to take her to work. She was this statuesque blond, so gorgeous it was hard for me to swallow when I looked at her. Bye was also taking her home from work. I know that, too, because he was regularly coming in dazed in the early morning hours, tripping over me sleeping on the floor of Hardin's apartment. We weren't getting in a lick of practice, but at the same time I wasn't really blaming Bye either. If I'd been a little younger I suppose the whole thing could have been hard to fathom, but I was old enough to be restless when Bye would come in smeared with lipstick and bearing the sweet fragrance of her perfume in the wee hours of the morning. It was tantalizing, I can tell you, and I was fast becoming aware that there was more to life than tennis.

"Still, I do admit to a certain bitterness of heart about what was happening. The thing we were supposed to be readying ourselves for, the Heart of America, seemed more remote with each passing day. Whenever I reminded Bye, he'd put me off with some alibi about the car needing work, though it was plain enough to me that it sat idle only because of his strong preference for Hardin's convertible.

"Then one night when I'd given up hope and resolved to hitchhike home, he came in late, woke me up and said, 'Let's go!' With only one day left before it was supposed to start, it seemed he'd at last remembered the tournament in Kansas City. It was the wildest thing I'd yet encountered. I mean there I'd been, full of tender hope and anticipation, and now here we were, neither of us having swung a racket since we'd left home, lighting out of Vegas at three a.m., trying to make up for two lost weeks in a day and a night. I didn't press Bye for explanations—he seemed nervous, cross, distraught. I wrote it off to another whirlwind romance that must have gone badly at the end. For the most part we rode in silence, but for a car that needed work the black Olds roared along like a thunderbolt.

"We drove without stopping except at these little combination gas station-grocery stores for gas, cookies and milk. I was dragged out and emaciated, and of course Bye wasn't any better off. He argued abruptly that we were in a hurry—an incredible, impossible hurry if he wanted the whole truth—although by then I suspected more compulsive motives: he wasn't one to spend a dime if he could help it. He held it close to eighty on those straight and lonely roads through eastern Colorado. When he was too tired to go on he'd give me the wheel and nap in the passenger's seat beside me—he wouldn't trust me with his car from the back seat. I remember that second morning found me headed straight into a big red sunrise in western Kansas, my bloodshot eyes hurting so that I could hardly face it.

"Tired as I was, there was something about the landscape that I've never gotten over. Not like the landscape around here, to be sure, but clean and open all the same. No mountains, but hills, rolling hills. And grass. It was something about the way the grass smelled, wet in the morning dew—against that red sun at dawn you could see the water droplets on the wheat and grass and even the fence posts. Or take the smell of the warm asphalt on a summer morning blending with it. When we stopped at these little service stations in the little towns and stood at the edge of the road, something in me unwound and relaxed luxuriously, I can tell you. Yes, people complain about the summer heat there, it's true, but get up early enough in the morning and it's a lovely heat. It'll warm your heart clear through.

"Something about those little towns, too. They sit out there on those plains all by themselves, peaceful and quiet. You come down the highway through nothing but wheat fields and after awhile you see another one, nestled in that undulating land beside a bend in the road, maybe, a vertical cluster of green trees, silos and water towers, the streets sometimes paved with brick.

"Well, gentlemen, it was in one of those little towns that it happened, the thing I was going to tell you about. We had almost passed through the town in question when Bye decided we needed some gas—I guess we almost missed the man, come to think of it. It's enough to make you believe in fate.

53

"Anyway, Bye made a U-turn, went back into town, and stopped at a small store that had a gas pump in front of it. Across the highway was a small park-like affair: a square of grass, a few shady elms, and a green bench where two old men were sitting. Bye disappeared behind the screen door which bore one of those metal crosspieces advertising Rainbow bread, raising a swarm of flies as he slammed it. While I bought the gas I noticed that one of the old men across the road had left his bench and started toward us. Bye came out with two Seven-Ups and a box of raisins, scattering flies again, and by the time the old fellow approached us we were ready to leave.

"I'd watched him crossing the highway, fascinated. Those small midwestern towns are the places to go if you're looking for characters. This one didn't exactly walk; he came sidling toward us like a wounded animal, his hand pressed near his groin—I thought at first he had to pee real bad and was in a race to the restroom. As I've said, he wore this green visor, wore it too low, it seemed, and tilted his head back to compensate like a man going under trying to keep his nose above the water, leading with this pointed wedge of a jaw. Oh yes, gentlemen, in your taxonomy of things, this was a geezer if there ever was one.

"He struggled up to us just as Bye closed the car door. Bye started the motor as if he hadn't seen him. His right hand still pressed to his groin, the old fellow swung a patched-up duffle bag from his shoulder with his left. His faded blue shirt was unbuttoned a little at the chest, revealing a soiled white undershirt. Brown, knotty forearms and knobby elbows were exposed below the rolled-up sleeves. His khaki pants, too short and baggy, were awkwardly bunched under a belt cinched desperately tight around his receding waist.

"When Bye started the car he stooped a little to peer in the window, pushing his visor around on his head like a baseball catcher, and I had my first good look at his face. His stubbled, jutting jaw was working with a nervous energy as if to worry a chew of tobacco, though I think it was just a habit, a kind of tic, I suppose. His ears protruded from his disheveled gray head and seemed to wiggle and dance. His brows, too, were busy, bushy and gray. Set in the webbed flesh above a pair of sun-rouged cheekbones, the eyes were twinkling merrily at us. I had the feeling he was definitely trying to charm us. Then he spoke.

"'You fellars headin' to Airzonie? I seen your plates an' was hopin' you might could help a fellar along.' The sound of his voice, thin and boyish, almost cracking, touched a nerve in me somewhere. I could have invited the poor old guy in and turned back toward home on the spot. Seeing Bye disdain, however, he came forth with an added appeal, still holding himself, wagging his head as he explained, like one veteran of the road to a knowing companion.

"'Been walkin' a fur piece today, and I'm bad hurt.'

"Bye finally looked at him, and when at last he spoke, his cruelty—so terribly uncalled for—surprised even me.

"'What's the matter, Pops,' he blurted. 'Somebody steal your truss?'

"The old man's jaw quit working and dropped open. He stared as if somebody had stung him. Bye gunned the car and circled out on the highway, heading east again, leaving the poor man standing there.

"I looked over my shoulder and watched him as long as I could. He stood squinting after us—it fairly wrung my heart, I can tell you. His jaw started slowly to work again, and he turned to the station attendant and said something as if in anger. Then he adjusted his visor, hoisted his bag again, turned his back on us and began to sidle on down the road toward 'Airzonie,' if that was really his destination. I saw him turn around one last time to look at us. He shook a fist, then turned his back again. It was the only time he'd lifted his hand from his groin.

"It's clear as yesterday when I get to talking about it. That incident has stayed with me all these years, and I believe it would have, too, even if what I'm going to relate hadn't happened.

"The thing is, gentlemen, he was like us in a way—more ways than one, perhaps. Oh, he was going one direction and we were going the other, to the Heart of America, true enough. But he didn't know that, and of course in his own way he was right, right as right can be, if you follow me. I'd never seen myself until the moment I saw that boyish twinkle in his eyes, heard that strangely boyish cackle. We were two young fellows off on a lark that wasn't panning out, and here was this old geezer going the other way who at heart was not much different. There's something there, to be sure—a certain grim parody, if you will...but now I'm saying too much, no doubt.

"'The downhill geezer,' Bye snorted, and he drove on in a sullen pout. I think he regretted what he'd done—it would have been easy enough to explain we were going the other way. It wasn't like him, really. Whatever else he was, he meant no harm. But from that moment on, in the summer I turned seventeen, I knew I'd lost an idol, and that was just the beginning of it all. In a way, I suppose, I'd gained something, too. Insight, call it. Too much insight. I won't say more about it.

"We were late to Kansas City, of course, and Bye didn't get the bye he had counted on. I could have told him there were no free passes where we were headed, though I wasn't sure just where that was. We'd both been defaulted. We read our names on the draw sheet, but that was all. We'd been there, to the Heart of America, and yet we hadn't.

"It was hot and humid and my clothes were sticking to me. We both needed a shave. I reflected that all we'd had to eat that day was a box of raisins and a Seven-Up apiece. I should have been hungry, but my stomach was in a knot and I had a bad taste in my mouth.

"'Hard luck,' I said to Bye.

"'Save it,' he snapped. 'I don't give a damn. Been losing all my life. Don't give a damn.'

"That wasn't like him either. I didn't know what he meant about losing all his life—just because for once he hadn't been lucky. I sat in the stands and watched awhile until it looked like it was going to rain. Bye came over and said 'Let's get the hell out of here.' I intended to concur, thinking he was referring to the rain.

"'Let's get some sleep,' I suggested.

"'Sleep in the car,' he snapped. 'I'm going home. You can come if you like, and if you want to know the truth, I don't give a damn.' He was already walking away when he said it.

"'Jesus,' I sighed out loud, and I fell in doggedly behind him.

"We didn't exchange a word for hours. I was too tired and too glum to talk, so I was just as glad we didn't. The rain had commenced, and in the dark that night we were driving into a heavy downpour somewhere on those rolling plains of western Kansas.

"It was along there that a couple of things happened, and I'm still not sure that the first was real. We shouldn't have even been on the road that night. You couldn't see twenty feet ahead of you except when lightning lit up the sky and a longer stretch of the road, which it did every now and then. Still, Bye crept on, pressing his face forward in grim perseverance while the windshield wipers labored at an impossible task.

"We were just topping a rise when lightning struck, casting a momentary greenish light like a short-fused flare.

"'Watch out!' I cried.

"I'll never know whether he saw what I saw, or whether what I saw was real. He wasn't speaking to me then—I guess I was on his nerves—and so neither of us ever said anything about it. He did swerve, though, and when I looked at him afterwards his hands were shaking on the wheel.

"What I'd seen, or thought I'd seen, was the drenched and improbable figure of a man. He was laboring up the hill on the roadside with something thrown over his back, and when he appeared, momentarily huge in that sudden burst of illumination, it seemed to me that he was dangerously close to our right fender. He wheeled around as we approached, lifting his right arm to us, and as he did so I could see he was no stranger to us. Yes, gentlemen, that was our 'downhill geezer'—the very same, unless my eyes deceived me. You'll say impossible to tell, and yet I could swear that his turning around like that revealed he was wearing a visor, and there, too, as we passed by within a foot of it, was that peculiarly mobile face with the working jaw. I swear, moreover, that it wasn't a thumb he thrust at us, but that same fist he'd scolded us with before—as if he'd somehow known it was us again.

"'Impossible,' you'll say, and surely you're right. Yes, I'll have to give you that. But do you know, to this day I have a thing about hitchhikers. Those arms, those faces by the roadside are cryptic symbols. They're road signs of the spirit—and the signs aren't good.

"By dawn I was sleeping fitfully in the back seat when a sharp jolt to my eardrums brought me wide awake. I thought we'd had a blowout, and said as much to Bye. The rain had ceased, and he was easing over to the muddy shoulder, not looking very good, staring with that same fixed gaze he'd been driving with when I fell asleep, but now he was staring at his hands instead of the road.

"'That was no blowout,' he muttered. 'We just drifted together. Like gravity.'

"You mean we were hit?"

"'It was as much my fault as his. I couldn't get off the centerline. It was like hypnosis.'

"'Jesus,' I fairly whistled. 'I better spell you awhile. We're lucky to be sitting here.'

"He pulled himself together and straightened up. 'You bet your ass we are,' he assured me, and he drove on down the road.

"We stopped soon for gas and I got out to check the damage done. In the side of the black Olds there was just a small dent the size of a pancake. It was real, though. It hadn't been there before, and there was a trace of red paint in it. When the attendant, a rotund little man in an engineer's cap, left off cleaning the windshield and hobbled around beside me to inquire, I explained we'd been tagged on the road by another car.

"'Boys, boys,' he sighed. He shook his head in a troubled way as he spoke and walked slowly back into the station. Him I'll remember almost as well as the geezer, and the sad intonation of that 'Boys, boys' is as real as here and now.

"To my surprise Bye pulled in at a motel on the edge of town. He was in a terrible blue funk and not speaking, so I went into the office myself. There was nobody there so I rang the bell on the counter, and after a minute a sunburned woman in shorts and a halter came in to wait on me. She warmed up and didn't seem to want to stop talking. A lonely woman, no doubt, who had seen better years. She was a little on the heavy side and yet not without a certain sensuous grace. She made me think of Donna Martel—'Donna Martel twenty years from now,' I thought to myself.

"She followed me to the door and stood smiling behind the screen while I explained to Bye that I'd arranged a room for us at day sleeper's rate. He looked up finally, and indicating with a glance the woman in the doorway, he complained in a grudging, terrible stage voice, 'At that price she ought to come with it.' The woman quit smiling and closed the door.

"So I went to sleep in a bed, finally. It was still morning but I didn't need any prompting. I remember I left Bye sitting up writing a letter. I didn't know it at the time but that morning was the beginning of the longest night of my life.

"I woke up at dusk to the insistent pounding of someone at our door. It was the woman who had checked us in, still in shorts but with a man's blue work shirt now covering the halter.

"'You boys have overslept,' she scolded me gently. 'I'll have to charge for the night unless...' She'd peered around me into the room and caught a hand to her mouth.

"My spine crawled, and I had a sudden knowledge of what I'd find even before I turned around, a premonition simultaneous with the woman's fiercely whispered, 'Oh my God! Oh my God!' as she hurried away up the graveled drive. The sheets and pillow of his coverless bed were fairly soaked, and Bye himself lay face down in the pillow. One limp forearm fell over the edge of the bed. It's sliced wrist, pitifully bruised and swollen, told the story.

"I spent a part of that night in the waiting room of a county hospital, gentlemen, though it was nothing like the one you behold here, and perhaps a better part of it in the sheriff's office, answering what questions I could, including one about the identity of a girl named Laurel Leroux. I confessed I probably knew her, if she was from Las Vegas, but not very well. It seems they'd found a letter addressed to her that they apparently thought explained a great deal. I asked if the letter would be mailed. They thought my question odd, and said 'Probably not.'

"And how much did I tell them of our two visitations, our erstwhile geezer, you may want to know? I thought to tell them, yes, but then I decided against it. For one thing, I didn't want to involve the old boy, but for another I gave no credence to any such thing as a curse. Still don't, to tell the truth. It's what's real that absorbs me, gentlemen, absorbs and appalls me both—why, there's the curse, come to think of it, and you don't have to look far...But I won't digress again, not now, anyway. At any rate, the curse of the downhill geezer, if you care to subscribe, was hardly a matter for the sheriff, but rather a private, moral matter—what I've called a road sign of the spirit, if indeed you subscribe to that entity, too.

"No, for all these years I've let the geezer be. Bye Johnson, too. I never brought up the name again until now—save once, which I'll come to shortly. He let his own blood in that room while I slept till the dusk had quietly gathered, my fallen idol whom I was detesting even while I slept, I believe. And, of course, he wasn't all that bad—I see that now—no worse than the rest of us by any honest man's standards. No, gentlemen, it's vanity for a man to judge another. We're all remarkably the same, if you ask me. Look long enough and hard enough and you can't help but see it. We've got our limits, every meat-eating daughter and son of us, and when it comes to handing out the laurels, the kind men think to praise one another with, I prefer to be somewhere else, for I'm likely to be sick. Better yet, I'll have a laugh and ridicule the bastards.

"Oh, I see your thoughts plain enough. Our humanist friend here will be asking me where my lantern is. But I'm no Diogenes, not me. Just something of a realist, as I've said—or so I'd counter if you pressed me.

"So it comes down to this, gentlemen...but no, the story doesn't end here and I'll finish it first. There's a kind of postscript, and I'll make it brief, as indeed it was.

"I hadn't been home long when I took a bus to Vegas to look up a girl named Laurel Leroux. It took some cheek for a girl-shy kid like me, but I had some vague notion about owing it to Bye Johnson, some explanation about the letter that was probably never sent. More likely that was some self-deception—as I've confessed, I was half in love with the girl myself.

"She wasn't in the book, and being on foot it took me a while to find what I thought was the apartment complex that I'd once been to with Bye. But I'm good at that sort of thing—have a sixth sense for it—and by the end of the day I'd found it. By then I assured myself that she wasn't in, so I didn't try to find out, but contented myself instead with the show at the Sands that night to see if she was still there. I learned nothing, of course. Even if a man were on the most intimate terms with a Vegas showgirl, I don't see how he'd know her on stage. In plumes and powder and lurid light they're every last one of them alike—like manikins, it occurs to you later.

"But morning light has a way of putting everything in its place, at least for me, and surprisingly I had no difficulty summoning the courage to push her doorbell several times in the midst of the morning that followed. If ever you love a showgirl, gentlemen, don't call on her in the morning, or you shan't be her caller again—by your choice, if not her own.

"I nearly apologized when the door opened, but thinking the woman who held it might be an older sister or even a mother, I ventured to inquire anyway.

"'I'm sorry ma'am. I was looking for Laurel Leroux.'

"'I'm her,' she assured me.

"Dumbfounded, I stood offering her the quart of milk I'd nearly tripped over, which she accepted without a trace of a smile.

"'This had better be good,' she warned. She made a tough, accusatory little gesture at me with her chin just to let me know she wasn't talking about the milk.

"I was trying to decide if this could be, and finally concluded that it could. She wore a white terrycloth robe that obscured her figure, but she had the stature all right, and she had the imperious, slightly raised chin of the showgirl on stage. It was her hair pulled tight on her head in curlers that made her so hard to recognize. It wasn't that she was ugly, not by ordinary standards, but standing there with her chin aloft in the hard, true light of morning, deprived of all make-up, she was simply plain, amazingly plain.

"'I'm a friend of Bye Johnson's.' I felt as though I was playing my last card in a very bad hand.

"'Who the hell is that?'

"'If she were only pretty, nothing more,' I couldn't help thinking, 'this would all be coming out better.' But this was the girl who had once been gorgeous, so utterly gorgeous I'd had to swallow hard at the sight of her. It was unreal. But no, this was real—it was the manikins that gave the world the lie.

"'He's nobody, ma'am. And I'm nobody too. Let's just forget I ever was.' I spoke instinctively—I couldn't think—and I turned and walked away.

"I walked for miles without stopping until I was on the Strip. Here, too, it struck me, was the heart of America, perhaps the real one. Oddly appropriate, the names of those places along the Strip. Sands, Dunes, Stardust. Something ephemeral about them all, don't you think? All that electricity, and still one of the dark places of the earth.

"That was what I wanted to say to all those elated visitors I passed, all those prancing tourists who cavorted in that artificial glow. But no, whenever I saw a party of merrymakers approaching, I wanted nothing better than to cross to the other side.

"Yes, gentlemen, I turned and walked away, and I've been walking ever since. Career, wife, family—'that whole catastrophe,' as Zorba had it—I've walked away from it all. Still, I won't be telling the truth if I don't add that the worst of it was I didn't give a tinker's damn when it came right down to it. I've lived since then without so much as what you'd call a friend. I've never said this before and I know what you're thinking. Yet it's the truth, gentlemen. Ask yourselves sometime when you're alone in the dark if it isn't. Oh yes, I've had chances enough, with women too, to be sure. 'It's like you're never really here,' one of them said to me once, and for the life of me it's as if I'm not. Always there's something in me that turns away. I'm nobody, I told her, and so I am, and the world of men's a hell of nothingness."

He faltered slightly, and Big Frank and I had time to exchange an uneasy glance, but only momentarily.

"I turned away, but I didn't care. That's been my curse, if it seems like that to you, gentlemen. I wouldn't know. I'm happy enough whenever there's an empty road before me. It's all I need and all I care for. And all of this I don't

60

need." He made a sweeping gesture with the pronouncement, taking in the New Paradise Inn, its terraced gardens and tennis courts, the lights from the city below us. "New Paradise—hah! A fool's paradise is what we have, and it's a downhill game to the end until we see it. Vanities, mere vanities, and nothing more, if we care to see the truth. That's my curse too, gentlemen...."

We sat in darkness, avoiding, I sensed, each other's imagined glances. After awhile three of us, like fugitives, rose one by one to leave. Flinders was left sitting there alone. From the poolside down below him I heard the woman's laughter treble gaily at the edge of the now darkened water.

Gleanings

At the top of the first stone buttress which supports the wall of the church, it appears to Graves that the cement-cast gargoyle is missing, although because it would be at the end of a row of them this is not immediately noticeable. When he walks by in the early morning he looks first for the pigeons which are often congregating on the crest of the pitched slate roof to catch the new sunlight, heedless of the aberrant inventions of humankind not far beneath them. Sadly, Graves can see that one of their number, ruffled and muddied, lies dead at the curbing. Their lugubrious chant seems fitting, while the gargoyles, with folded wings and heedless in turn, extend their sleek necks and heads to gaze at the street below in mindless delight.

Except for Graves the street is deserted. In summer, though the Church of the Nativity is no longer in use, it is not unusual for him to see visiting tourists appraising the premises with camera in hand. Sensing that he must belong to the small western city he walks, they will sometimes inquire of him for directions, which in some slight way he is always gratified in giving. He once traveled widely for his living, but now a widower, he stays close to home and asks nothing more of his remaining years than peace and quiet. Even when both elude him, however, he finds he can still take heart in the smallest gestures of goodwill and civility.

Now at summer's end the prevailing quiet is only deepened by the mourning pigeons, and yet Graves has reason to distrust his hearing. He lives just a block, as the crow flies, from a large high school, and each fall he is entertained, like it or not—and Graves tries hard to like it—by the brassy blare of a marching band as they practice close by but out of sight on the school's football field. Possibly it has been a phenomenon prompted by just such circumstances, but during the summer something quite remarkable was occurring, causing him to pause, cock his head slightly and listen intently. He could not be sure, but it sounded like the music of a band that he was hearing, a marching band, though thus out of season for the one he was accustomed to, and marching in his direction, too, for the sound seemed always to swell in volume while he listened.

His perceptions could at first be easily enough explained, being attributable to nothing more than the emanations from some downtown festivity, on which occasions, perhaps two or three times a summer, amateur bands did indeed play and sometimes parade to entertain the city's visitors. Yet as the summer progressed Graves found the experience recurring at least weekly. Moreover, the music that reached his hearing seemed sublime. He could only conclude that the band he heard played not only with inordinate skill but with their whole hearts, for their renditions were truly arousing, beginning always faintly but carefully building to the most compelling crescendos, and eventually bringing him to his curb to peer down the long block he lived on to where it seemed the source of this enchantment was about to round the corner and come marching up the street to him.

But always the wonderful sounds stopped short, and the band, if there was one, never appeared. Graves was left to assume that he suffered from auditory illusions, though the possibility failed to disquiet him. With school resumed, he now listens again to the real band as it rehearses on the nearby field. The illusions have ceased, and, though still distrustful, he gives them no further thought.

Early in October, when he first sights the man, Graves is perched on his stool at the window of the Station House, having his morning coffee and just finding his place in the book he carries. Distracted, he glances up to see a well dressed man in a light top coat, British tan, and a derby hat—a professional of some sort, he infers, but someone he has never noticed before. He gives him no further thought until he arrives again from the direction in which he has passed, but this time he pauses to scan the sidewalk up and down, then studies the far side of the street as if seeking an address, or perhaps merely trying to get his bearings. Graves has a good look at him. He sees an unassertive mustache, well kept and graying, a neatly knotted tie, and in the band of the derby a modest little feather. Tall and rather slender, the man looks to be about the same age as Graves, who is sixty-nine. When he turns and begins to walk away, dropping his gaze, Graves can see that his chin is slightly receded and his cheeks a little hollow. His eyes look pale and forlorn, and his whole demeanor is that of a man given to indecision and introspection.

After this first encounter days go by before Graves sees the man again, but throughout the fall, as the days turn gradually colder, he keeps appearing at random until Graves begins to watch for him. As he makes his morning treks to the Station House, the man has a way of appearing in his vision at one point or another, perhaps well in front of him on the sidewalk, or passing on the opposite side of the street, always in the tan top coat, perhaps with a lining now buttoned into it to judge from the heavier way it has begun to enclose him. Once in a while he is hatless, as if the derby has been forgotten, but he has taken to wearing an expensive looking pair of brown leather gloves. Pausing, as he is still wont to do, he will let his hands dangle as if from the weight of them, hesitate, then give his arms a little penguin-like flap against the slightly increased bulk of his coat, and make his worried way in the opposite direction.

Aside from the tourists, there are also the transients to be observed on the streets, especially in summer, but also in the fall while the weather holds. One morning when Graves arrives one of them is seated in the Station House, wearing a heavy cable knit sweater, soiled and frayed, mumbling incoherently to anyone who will listen—Graves is able to catch accusatory phrases about a war somewhere and, surprisingly, about "the disappearing middle class." His hair matted and his face flushed, he keeps standing up beside his stool and holding aloft various coins which he fishes from the pockets of his greasy levis, turning slowly as though inviting all to observe, and giving Chad, the young counterman, cause for concern.

Graves leaves before witnessing the outcome, but he knows it is not unusual for such drifting personages to hang around for days before disappearing, their unwelcome presence perceived as a threat and strained contrast to that of the summer vacationers who dine at their leisure in the best restaurants and out on the open patios. Their few possessions, if any, are packed on their backs or toted in plastic sacks which serve as makeshift luggage. Sometimes they travel in pairs and gabble at one another, but Graves has come to suspect that such pairings are also makeshift and, like themselves, transitory. More often they wander alone, though he has noticed that this does not necessarily inhibit the tendency toward conversation, whether with themselves or the world at large, which often as not rises to an argumentative pitch.

Graves wonders whether the solitary older man he is now always watching for could be one of them. Probably not, he reasons, for his gentlemanly appearance sets him apart, and perhaps even more telling, there is that touch of anxiety in his erratic wanderings which reminds Graves of a lost dog.

Then, glancing back while he walks in a November dawn, he perceives that the man is not far behind him—within earshot, surely, for he feels his disappointment as he overhears the threads of a conversation in progress. Still, he consoles himself with the observation that the monolog is not unseemly, the words, as far as he can discern, free from profanity and incrimination, the volume controlled. Graves, for his own part, must admit that he occasionally catches himself enunciating some word or phrase aloud when alone.

He has finished his coffee and turned his first corner on the way home when suddenly he beholds the man again, this time loitering on the corner at the end of the block. But no, it is wrong to think he loiters, for he seems possessed again by that vague anxiety, hesitant, twirling his coat as he surveys his alternatives before striking out again, lifting a hand to the rim of his derby to shade his eyes as he turns them east toward Graves. While he is closing the space between them, Graves realizes they are about to pass on the same side of the street, for the object of his attention has begun to amble in his direction.

Intuitively, Graves knows better than to look too soon directly at the man, for he senses something fragile about him—not shyness, exactly, but something elusive, a propensity for avoiding further contact, perhaps, if approached too abruptly. He tries to appear nonchalant, but just as they meet, with all the care that he can summon he looks into the passing face and pronounces his "Good morning," extending what he hopes is all goodwill and warmth in the early morning sunlight. The man's glance slides across his own, registering for just the briefest instant, he thinks, consternation, but in the same instant recovering to offer the faintest of smiles and even to nod. As seems his habit, he drops his countenance and passes without a hitch in stride, yet not before Graves has detected a soft but clearly spoken "Morning," which then resounds over and again to him as he makes his way homeward. Although he cannot be sure, he is tempted to believe that this fortuitous exchange has been the result of something other than mere chance.

"Little shits shouldn't be allowed to drive a car, if that's the best they can do with it." His neighbor, fetching his morning paper, is trying to make conversation with him as Graves passes by, and he refers to the raucous rap of the teenagers who cruise this street near the high school with their radios throbbing, as one of them just has, even before the sun is up. Graves understands the man's annoyance.

He offers a tentative nod, smiling, but in truth he is not really sure what to make of it. He could move, of course. He has been down to Phoenix and Tucson and seen the various Sun Cities to be had there. Yet in the early mornings he passes the school parking lot and sometimes exchanges a greeting with the first of the arriving teachers, for whom he has come to hold unspoken respect, and he has decided to stay where he is. He tries instead to understand. Perhaps the urgent diatribes let loose on the streets are the poetry otherwise missing from their lives, and from what he can make of them they invariably take the form of protest. It is a form to be encouraged, perhaps, for it seems to him there is much to protest. Out on the interstates, back when he traveled for his living, he encountered epidemic violence, so that he once constructed a set of large white cards with bold black numbers—"65," "55," even a "45," for construction zones—and carried these reminders in the seat beside him, intending them for use on his fellow motorists. In the end, however, he thought better of it, and he never displayed them.

Now at the end of the block a youth in a souped up low-rider careens around the corner, rubber squealing. He sees Graves staring, flips him a finger, and opens the throttle, doing what Graves takes to be a hundred down the street. Graves hopes he doesn't kill someone, or someone's dog. He recalls a dog he once observed in Phoenix, some years ago, when headed homeward in the roiling traffic of the urban freeway. It was midsummer, and in the scant shade of some portable concrete barriers left along the median, something caught his eye. Turning to look, he saw a stray dog, mistaking him at first for a coyote—which he resembled, save for his darker and brindled coloring. Reclining against a barrier in the cramped safety zone of the median, he lifted his head to stare calmly at nothing in particular, sphinx-like, while the traffic raged around him. It occurred to Graves to ease over and stop, to find somehow a break in the traffic and cross to the median, if all of that were possible, but even then, he foresaw, there would be the difficulty in approaching a dog like that, taking refuge where he had, at home in the eye of the storm.

What a state the world is in, Graves thinks, and in truth, again, he suspects he is witness to the beginnings of a vast and unnamable deterioration, the causes of which are no longer debated or railed about. Yet they are nothing he likes to dwell upon, for he cannot think how he has ever raised a hand against them.

It is that same morning that Graves, seated in the hole-in-the-wall Station House, feels himself making his first mistake with regard to the newcomer who has taken to pacing the streets where he himself indulges in his daily walks.

"There stands our newest citizen," he announces to Chad, who is straightening some stools beside him at the window. The words slip out as if he were thinking aloud, and yet he continues, if only by way of explanation to Chad, who now stands watching. With a nod he indicates the well dressed man in the tan overcoat standing opposite them across the street, as if searching for address numbers on their side of the passing traffic, but looking a little bewildered.

"I've been seeing him around. Fascinating character." Forcing a smile, he adds, "He's a symbol of sorts, I suppose."

Chad smiles, too. "Vibes," he offers, and Graves senses the cogency of this brief summation.

As they speak, the subject of their observations begins to cross the street. Dodging traffic, glancing when he can toward their window, he gains the near sidewalk and presents himself before the framed glass door. Just as he extends an arm, however, he draws back as though unsure of himself, reconsiders, then turns on his heels and disappears down the sidewalk.

To his quick regret Graves realizes that he and Chad, forgetting themselves along with another person or two, were staring at precisely the wrong moment. Something tells him he should never have spoken aloud of his new friend—for such is the manner in which Graves has begun to conceive of this man who, he must concede, remains a stranger to him. Now, he fears, he might be gone for good.

Two days pass which seem to confirm his premonition, but during the next morning the man comes pacing by the window of the Station House, just in the place Graves first glimpsed him. He almost misses him, for this time he is not only bareheaded, with hair slightly mussed in the breeze, but armed only with a brown leather jacket against the cold. His hands are thrust into his pockets, and his face is inclined forward in that familiar attitude which betrays his perplexity. Graves, a little surprised to notice how his heart has accelerated, finishes his coffee and takes to the sidewalk behind him.

At the nearest intersection he can see that halfway up the block, where the sidewalk is closed by a construction project, his would-be acquaintance is standing alone, hands still in pockets, apparently considering his alternatives. Graves proceeds slowly and is careful not to stare. The man has turned to peruse the window of the department store beside them, and Graves must address his back.

"Good morning," he offers, in the friendliest voice he can summon.

The man turns, this time as if expecting him, responds again with his clearly spoken "Morning," allows his not unfriendly glance to slide quickly over Graves once more, and then seems to search the distance down the street with eyes that fix themselves just above Graves' shoulder.

"Can I buy you a cup of coffee?" Graves pursues.

The man glances briefly into his face again—this time, Graves thinks, with sadness and perhaps the faintest trace of gratitude showing—and then looks back down the street.

"I have to wait for someone," he explains, and then begins to retrace his steps away from the construction site.

"Some other time," Graves suggests, by way of parting.

On the long walk home he considers again the man's last words, which led him to assume that he was waiting for a ride, for someone to pick him up, but now it seems to Graves that this was never likely, for the man was always alone. Graves begins to realize there is something about him—the gaunt cheeks when he pauses to take his bearings, the eyes that search the distance as if with expectation—that reminds him of someone, but someone he cannot put his finger on, and in the midst of this reflection he realizes, too, with certain knowledge, that he will never see the man again.

During the ensuing months Graves keeps an eye out for the man, though he knows in his heart it is useless. More fruitful are the reveries he finds himself indulging in throughout the meditative days of winter. Strange, he sometimes thinks, the things the memory chooses to retain. In the year of his retirement, for instance, he joined an alumni tour and went ten days to western Ireland, and the incident which stood foremost in his memory, to be retained above all else, seemed surely odd and possibly even insignificant.

Almost everywhere one looked there seemed to be a castle or an abbey, most in some stage of ruin but a few of them restored, and each day they were bused to one or another of them from their accommodations in the small city of Ennis, in County Claire. He watched the surf breaking on ancient cliffs, wondered at the neatly maintained homes and farms in their green landscapes, and yet what absorbed him most were the people themselves, their good nature and kindliness, but sometimes, too, if he passed them walking alone on the sidewalks of Ennis or some other town, their faces seemed touched with some distant melancholy even as they smiled at him.

At the end of their final day, returning to the outskirts of Ennis, his gaze fell upon the solitary figure of a man in the street where it curved and descended slightly between trim row houses and joined the thoroughfare where their bus was just then slowly passing. It was also the end of the summer, and the sun was almost done with what had been an overcast and drizzly day, but where the top of the street formed a part of the horizon the sky was soft and momentarily luminous. The man was a good half-block away, but as he lifted his face to them Graves still thought he could detect that faintly melancholy smile, and for reasons he could not have explained he sensed his identity with this man who strolled alone in the September twilight, knowing also in that same moment that whenever he recalled his first and probably only trip abroad this was the incident which would come first and last to mind.

With the coming of winter Graves retrieves the battered wood and plexiglass bird feeder from his shed and hangs it in the crab apple tree just off the front porch. Close by, he leaves the brass wind chime hanging throughout the year, taking care to keep it untangled.

Often the days are still warm, and he likes to retire to his study where the door opens onto the porch, allowing him to observe the tree with its feeder and the thick privet hedge beyond. He sees sparrows, finches, a few pine siskins and, smallest of all and arriving only in winter, hooded juncos with white bands in their tail feathers. Occasionally, too, there are boisterous visits from stellar jays, but of them all Graves is fondest of the sparrows, who seem content to winter in his hedges with their spontaneous comings and goings.

There is a magical hour late in the afternoons when they gather in the cover there and make their erratic sorties to the feeder and back, when their gentle whistlings and whirrings awake in him a sense of quiet elation while, from behind his screen door, he sits silently watching. They brake and hover at the feeder while the sun goes down behind the hedge, and there are frozen moments when the feathered workings of their wings and tails are transparent in the light. Graves thinks of angels, though he gives no more credence to such entities than he gives to the gargoyles whose representations are preserved for him on the walls of the church.

On New Year's Day the Station House is closed, but by noon, the day turning warm, Graves wanders out all the same to stroll downtown. He passes by the high school football field where a pick-up game of tag football is just under way. There are eight youths, four of them in blue jerseys, who look to be college age. Their voices are bright in the sunshine. Graves himself, however, retains little interest in such sport, and walks on by, but not before some fragment of a memory begins to stir.

He was sitting with his mother, who was young and beautiful, in a car parked among a row of them at the end of such a field. His father, who taught at one of the high schools and also coached the football team, was not there with them. There was a red team and a blue team, which only now and then attracted his attention. If he stood up in the seat he could see them scrimmage in the distance, but once (and this is the part that jogs Graves' memory) they all seemed to be running toward the goal post he and his mother were parked behind, chasing the ball which bounded loose upon the turf, and some of them came so close he could see their faces beneath their helmets.

Then for a little while the two teams left the field, and something wonderful began to happen. There was music which was growing louder—beautiful music, it seemed to him—and rows of people in red uniforms with broad white straps across their chests came marching toward them. His mother told him this was the band, and they both got out and sat on the hood of the car in order to see better. The band drew closer to them, their music gaining volume, and out in front of them was the thing that fascinated him most: a man, dressed all in gleaming white, was leading them. He wore a tall white hat with a bill which shaded his upturned face and his knees pumped high as he marched, while his white-gloved fist held something flashing silver—a baton, his mother said—which he also pumped up and down. But just as he neared the goal post he suddenly halted, and immediately the band also halted and broke off playing. He blew a blast on a whistle he brought to his lips with his free hand, and they all turned abruptly around. Then the leader pranced quickly through the waiting ranks until he was in front of them again, whistled a second time, and they all marched away back down the field, playing something new.

Their music died away and eventually stopped, and they all left the field at the far end where they had first assembled. The two teams came straggling back onto the field, and he thought he could just make out his father, whom his mother pointed out, walking briskly behind the blue team.

Later, after the game, he was standing in the seat between the two of them while his father drove, and in the back seat sat a player they were taking to his home, a player named Earl Canterbury (the name, strangely, still came back to Graves, though there might now be none to speak it). His helmet was placed on the seat beside him, and his hands and neck, protruding from his blue jersey, looked thick and strong. His sandy hair was damp and plastered to his forehead, and there was blood on the side of his face. Glancing around at him, he was aware that this was someone his father liked and esteemed.

"Did he like the game?" his father asked of his mother.

"He loved the band," his mother replied. "And he thinks he wants to be a drum major." His father turned his head to assess them both, then slowly smiled.

Wakeful at night, Graves considers whether he is a part of the disappearing middle class and hears the lonely wailing of freight trains which pass through the darkened city. Is it age, he wonders, or his want of employment now which brings him to this heady awareness of his own aloneness? Then he is lulled by the softer sound of the wind chime not far removed from his window left ajar, or of tires on the pavement just beyond, sometimes splashing lightly in the rain which by morning will have turned to snow.

On certain mornings in January he might wake to find his shrubs and hedges bent under the heavy whiteness, a branch from the silver maple already broken by the weight. Snow might still be falling and swirling, and the tops of the tall bare poplars behind his neighbor's home across the street still tossing in the unsettled air. There will be beauty in the scene beyond his window, yet he will not look forward to the wintry walk that awaits him. All the same, he will bundle up and go, taking care to wear shoes with good traction. His feet have more than once gone out from under him in such conditions, but he has learned to take his time and glance occasionally toward the mountains behind him. They might be veiled in snow and cloud, and when he gets downhill as far as the church they will be hidden from view, but he can be reasonably sure they are there, whether he sees them or not.

By February there are days which promise the spring, intermittent days when he wakes to the goodwill of a robin, perched somewhere in the still barren trees in his yard, singing in the dawn. Every year, it seems he tends to forget there will be such mornings, but always the first such occurrence is both new and familiar. He will rise and walk and from blocks away he will hear the piercing call of the flickers, who have stayed through the winter, he knows, but who choose to announce their presence only on such mornings as these. Such mornings as these, Graves reflects, when the air in his room with the window ajar is imbued with warmth and light and the cheer of birdsong.

Early in the morning on the third day of spring, Graves sights a dog running loose in the street up ahead. Tan with black marking, middle-sized, it summons to memory a dog from his boyhood. It disappears, but then it is back, closer now and pacing at an anxious trot. Like the dog he remembers, it is a short-haired male of obviously mixed breed, and the tops of the ears flop forward. Obviously, too, the dog is lost or abandoned. Spotting Graves alone on the sidewalk, he falls in behind him and begins to follow—Graves is familiar with the maneuver, other dogs having followed him in like manner. He thinks better of offering encouragement and walks steadily on, but the dog trots faithfully at his heels as though trying to pass himself off as a friend of long standing.

They are soon downtown together, but just as they near the Station House the dog is distracted by a pigeon foraging at the curbing close by. He gives chase just as Graves is entering. Perched on his stool at the plate-glass window, Graves can see his erstwhile companion pacing anxiously in the street once more—looking for him, he knows.

But the dog has vanished, to his relief, by the time he gets up to leave. Still, his relief is not uncomplicated. He is beginning his seventy-first year, as it happens, and he has declined this offer of friendship—from a would-be friend, moreover, who reminds him of one long ago. In the mornings that follow he looks in vain for him, and at the end of a week he determines he will drive out to the animal shelter, on the far side of town, for a look around.

Graves has never visited a prison, yet on his visit to the animal shelter he feels immediate empathy with the impounded dogs—something like a deja vu experience, he considers, though he has never before had occasion to take the concept seriously. There is even a metal door which slams behind him as he enters the area where four rows of cages, some forty-eight of them altogether, await his inspection.

Hesitantly, he makes his way before them, attempting to avoid contact for too long with eyes that beseech him, though some are not without suspicion and fear, or even rage—one dog, seemingly almost feral, leaps at the door of his cage to get at him as he passes. Yet near the end of his tour his gaze alights on a sight which gives him pause. Trembling and cowed in the shadows at the back of its cell, there crouches an animal looking so despondent that he fears for its survival—a young female shepherd mix, a nameless stray according to the card on her cage, perhaps part greyhound or whippet, he thinks, to judge by her thinness. For just a moment she returns his gaze, revealing eyes not so much pleading as deeply hurt, but then she quickly averts them, allowing them to close as she lowers her head, and Graves is stung to the heart by the gesture.

So it is that Graves, seeking one dog without success but in the process stumbling upon another, is back at the pound in another day, yet only to discover, as the heavy door slams shut behind him once again, that the cage he seeks is now deserted.

"It's a shame, but we have to do it," the attendant out in the lobby informs him. "We just don't have room for everybody." While Graves is reflecting on this usage of the "everybody," the man attempts a further justification. "When they're sick and obviously not going to make it. Sometimes also if they're mean and aggressive." The dog that leaped and lunged at Graves is also gone.

Then, while standing outside in the open air, he notices that four or five youths who have arrived in a church van are now walking some of the dogs, and it occurs to him that all of this was somehow meant to be. He completes the necessary form for volunteering, and he soon finds himself wandering the wooded hills outside the pound with a grateful dog on the end of his leash. He also finds that by arriving at opening hour, nine in the morning, he has time to take out three dogs, spending almost an hour with each. He is asked not to come on weekends, the busiest days for adoptions, but as a new world begins to open to him he increases his visits from once to twice a week.

The nights are shorter now and turning warmer. Wakeful again, Graves thinks he has heard someone yelling in the street outside, though at first he cannot be sure. Then he hears it again, farther up the street, and someone yells back, still farther away. There is an adolescent waver in their voices, and it is well past midnight. A couple of youths, he concludes, out on the prowl.

He recalls a motel in Denver where he sometimes stayed, an older, two-storied place which had seen better days—the kind of place in which he often found himself accommodated back in his days on the road. Upon his last stop there he was troubled at finding it enclosed by a chain-link fence, topped with barbed wire. Construction, he assumed, but then he began to understand that the former apartment buildings behind it were now a housing project of some sort. The buildings looked worn and prematurely aged, and from his upstairs room he could observe the comings and goings, mostly on foot, of the poor who now resided there. Late that night he was awakened by a gang of youths—both black and white, as well as he could determine—gathered at the fence, hurling their threats and insults. Graves watched warily, thinking himself undetectable in his darkened room, and yet one of the smaller boys seemed to be staring directly and furiously at him. He stooped to pick something up, cocked his arm and hurled his missile, whatever it was, unmistakably at Graves' window. Involuntarily, Graves ducked, though apparently nothing was actually thrown.

The animal shelter, in a clearing of ponderosa pine among similarly wooded foothills on the far edge of the city, is accessible only by a mile of unpaved washboard road, hook-shaped, which ends abruptly by climbing the little knoll where the shelter is secluded. Between the hills are narrow, dry meadows where prairie dog towns are thriving. When Graves walks far enough in any direction he can see the grand suburban homes which ring the area, and he can hear an unseen bulldozer in the hills beyond, no doubt clearing space for more of them. It seems to him that there are nevertheless countless trails through the nearer hills awaiting his discovery. Some of these, faint and barely traceable, he takes to be pathways worn upon the land by the area's wild inhabitants, and it is in ascending these through brush and around rocky outcroppings that he and his canine companions have come upon the elk and white-tailed deer who must have made them. On three occasions, too, Graves thinks he has seen a coyote—a stealthy, almost spectral presence, keeping its distance but each time watching them, and then reluctantly retreating. Whether or not it is the same coyote, sighted on separate days, Graves has no way of knowing.

At such encounters the dogs will sometimes pull and rear, but more often they stand and gaze, spellbound, like Graves himself. They often begin their walks with such eagerness as to pull him off balance at his end of the leash, but invariably they return at a more docile pace with their tongues dangling.

"That time on the leash is good for them," he is told one morning by Peg, a member of the staff who comes out on her break for a smoke. All of them have grown used to seeing him there, and he is sometimes thanked for his services. "Whatever you're doing, it's working for them."

The reference, he knows, is to the fact that the dogs he walks are frequently adopted. They recognize him when he enters, and unable to disappoint them, he tends to take the same dogs out again until, arriving of a morning, he finds them missing. He turns to a new one among those he has neglected, regretting, always, the limitations imposed by his fatigue, and then the sequence has a way of repeating itself.

They are treated humanely, as far as he can discern, yet he cannot overcome the feeling on his visits that he is an emissary from the outside world to the imprisoned, a few of whom seem to bear the weight of a death sentence. But even though most have been incarcerated through no fault of their own, Graves is able to read forgiveness and longing in their eyes, eyes which seem, moreover, incapable of dissembling, their emotions being always transparent.

Indeed, as he eases along the rough dirt road toward the graveled parking lot of the shelter, Graves has only to lower his window to comprehend the anguish within its walls, from which the pitched and plaintive vocalizations, the long moans and the drawn out howls, seem always audible and consummately expressive.

Late in May, on a blustery morning when the wind feels warm, Graves has just emerged from the downtown streets and undertaken the ascent beyond the church, where the sidewalk rises perhaps fifty feet in the course of a block, when he realizes he is not going to make it—not without resting, at any rate. Whereas he ordinarily welcomes the daily ritual of his heart and lungs contending with this modest resistance, his legs are now leaden, and there is a pain near the center of his chest which he has been gradually forced to acknowledge—and which is finally sharp enough to bring him to a halt. Seating himself on a little retaining wall which withholds the sloping yard of a bed and breakfast inn, he feels the pain spread through his shoulders and arms, so that even his hands feel dilated and heavy. He hasn't been sleeping well, and a great fatigue consumes him. Resting with elbows on knees and face in his cupped hands, he waits. The pain seems long in subsiding, but when at last it does he stands and slowly straightens himself, then labors with great care until he has surmounted the small hill.

Thinking about the experience during the remainder of the day, he wonders a little that it fails to trouble him, that even at the time it caused him no alarm. If he was not mistaken, he saw the curtains part in an upstairs window of the inn, where a woman watched while he endured his pain. Rising, he glanced up again and saw her vanish with a smile of what seemed recognition. Someone he should have known, perhaps, though he cannot think who.

By midsummer Graves has detected no sign of the band music which distracted him the previous year, though at times, working in his yard, he has stood still to listen. Nor can he recall without some omissions by then the dogs that he has walked and tried to befriend, a circumstance which he regrets, particularly in the case of those who were never spoken for.

He is aware, however, that there is usually a dog who is foremost in his thoughts on the days between his visits, a dog he will be glad to get back to, knowing he will be missed. At present it is a rangy, youthful Doberman mix of cheerful disposition, black and caramel-colored, whom someone has named Snickers. Since their first walk together he recognizes Graves at once when he enters, rears up gently against the front of his cage as if making sure he will not go unnoticed, and, ears back and stubby tail wagging, attempts to put his best foot forward. Graves obliges by going straight to him, even though he might subsequently have to pass his cage with another dog in tow. Yet Snickers seems incapable of resentment or any ill will toward man or dog.

Just now, as Graves pauses to catch his breath, Snickers pauses to inquire, turns and rears up tentatively on him, looks him in the face with his ears laid back and his orange eyes beaming. Graves senses that he is being offered an invitation, an unspoken proposal that they share their lives as companions, and he is intensely aware that the dogs are living beings like himself, his equals, for he has never thought of a dog as a pet, nor of himself as a master.

More than once the possibility of becoming an adopter has crossed his mind, but he has managed to think better of it, preferring to remain the volunteer walker he has become. Then one morning, before he can inquire, he is informed that Snickers has been adopted. He is relieved, as always, but saddened too—he will miss him. He turns his attention to those that remain and those who are new, resigning himself. It is all a part of some cycle, he prefers to think, beyond his own control.

"Some of the nicest people I know are dogs," he confides to Chad one morning, not a little surprised at the conviction in his voice.

Chad gives him a look, then smiles and nods, but whether in true agreement or out of mere politeness Graves cannot ascertain.

Another month has passed, however, when Graves first encounters the dog who will come to be most on his mind. He has just returned a white bull terrier to her cage near the end of the last aisle, his third dog of the morning, and preparing to leave, he hears a barely audible whine, a small complaint which is almost a sigh, not unlike the way his back screen door has begun to squeak, full of pain and longing.

"Well, hello there," he intones, stooping to peer into the adjacent cage where a great shaggy stray, collared with a piece of chain, lies watching him. His tail slowly thumping, the dog gets unsteadily to his feet as Graves eases into the cage and fastens the leash he carries to the chain. He pets the side of the inmate's shoulder, as is his habit, for reassurance, but he feels the big dog tremble slightly beneath his hand.

Outside he replaces the chain with a nylon collar and stays the extra hour to walk with "Woolly," as he calls him for want of anything better. Subdued and bedraggled, the dog walks slowly, and twice they must pause for his bouts of coughing and choking. Still he seems grateful, glancing back frequently at Graves as if in disbelief. And so begins for Graves the last great love of his life.

At home, hearing his screen door creak, he is smitten with sudden compassion. He increases his visits to three days a week, going first of all to "Willy," as he alters the name just slightly. His condition seemingly on the mend, Willy has a way of sauntering now as he walks slowly and close to Graves, his spine and hindquarters weaving gracefully, suggesting a cautious optimism.

Though he hazards no guess as to the mixture of his lineage, Graves finds his new friend beautiful, with woolly flop-over ears and a heavy but well shaped muzzle which finds its way disarmingly into his lap whenever he sits to rest. On such occasions he reaches over Willy's back in a kind of hug and pets his shoulder and flank, feels his heated breathing despite his deliberate pace, the metabolism burning faster than his own, then scratches behind and between the ears where the fur is dense but not so long. When he allows his hand to rest, the dog's eyes, hazel and glowing warm, roll around and seek his own. He has only to lower his face to feel his cheek caressed by Willy's tongue.

One morning in their third week together Graves pauses without sitting down, having overheard something delicate and arresting, perhaps the carole of the Western Tanager, or even the soft but surreal song of the Western Bluebird—wonderful birds, both, though he seldom hears and even more rarely sees them. He listens, and he realizes that what he hears is a human voice, pitched high and clear, a woman singing. He follows in pursuit, taking Willy with him over an unfamiliar trail, the intermittent refrains which reach them sweet but seemingly no closer. At length, topping a hill, they look down upon the glint of the morning sun on a bicycle—pushed along by the singing girl who is dressed in shadowless white, her long hair shining. As they watch she disappears in a pool of shade, beyond which the path bends out of sight.

They follow and reach the bend where the girl has vanished, but the singing has long since ceased. The trail forks, they can see, and the one Graves knows they should take is blocked, in part, by a token barricade of stones. He halts again. It is not the stones—there seems room to pass around or even between them—but the whitewashed warning he has read on them which gives him pause: "Never...Death...No Hope...Stay Away," he reads again. He is not superstitious, he reminds himself, but he considers Willy, who is looking up at him and patiently waiting. He hesitates, then leads Willy around the stones, and eventually, on a trail they at last come upon which he recognizes, back to the pound.

Graves is awakened that night by the barking of a dog at some distance down his block—a small dog, it sounds like, though one which he cannot identify. It is just past one o'clock, and he listens for the disturbance he suspects he will be hearing in the street, and yet he hears nothing. The barking has stopped, but he goes to the window to look. The street is empty, and the silence seems absolute. He can see the thin sliver of the moon overhead, and, closely aligned, a remarkably bright planet.

Graves returns to his bed but remains awake. Arriving with the mail that afternoon was one of his stories, rejected again. He has considered altering the title, replacing "The Westward Inn" with "The Westward End," a notion which has often troubled him, but he now decides he will send it out again just as it is, if only to find it a home. But as for "The Hadleyburg Renaissance," he has conceded it will remain always homeless, unknown to the world—save to himself, as a sad reminder of his inability to make it right.

It no longer seems to matter about writing such fictions, and he suspects that this has to do with the peace he finds in watching the birds in his hedges. He suspects, also, that the planet he has seen is Jupiter, but he has never known much about the heavens, and so cannot be sure.

On what turns out to be their final walk together Graves takes Willy to the hill where he has often seen the elk, an area he has avoided since the rutting season, but the season is by now well past, and he knows Willy to be too gentle to make trouble.

The narrow path they use, requiring a gradual ascent, is shaded most of the way for them. They see no elk, but when they have gained the clearing at the crest of the hill he detects some movement near the forest's edge, and there, within perhaps fifty yards of them, he counts six white-tailed deer as they bound gracefully away in the mottled light between the trees. He stops, kneels, and tries to point for Willy, who also stops and then stares as one and then a second straggler go bounding to catch up with the others, all of whom then fade from their view, deeper into the forest. It seems to Graves that he and the dog he kneels beside, in their moment of observing together beneath the late September sun, are in some way a single entity, transfixed and yet transported. When the deer are gone Willy looks at him with eyes reflecting wonder and gratitude, and together they resume their walk, following the dog's slow, sauntering pace.

On their return, at the mouth of a descending draw, they pause in the shade of a mountain cottonwood where, by one route or another, Graves has taken to resting. There, with himself settled on a well placed rock and his friend's quiet head at rest across his thigh, they can survey the longest of the meadows with its wildflowers—yellow penstemmon, purple lupine, Queen Anne's lace—swaying among the sunlit grasses and weeds. At some point, the compassion he has felt for the animal he holds has turned to love, and, momentarily, he rests at peace in the knowledge that his love is requited.

"Good boy," Graves whispers. "Yes, you are a good boy."

At home with the weekend before him, he recalls how each time he returns Willy to his cage the dog, though always obedient, hesitates just long enough to search his face, and Graves can no longer bear it. He doubts that any intervening adoption is imminent in the case of Willy, but by Sunday evening he determines that he will take Willy home with him, and his decision, once made, lifts his heart to an unforeseen lightness.

Yet he drives to the shelter on Monday morning with growing misgiving until, standing at last before what has been Willy's cage, he confronts the realization of his dread: in the place of his friend are two small newcomers huddled together in troubled sleep, the new card on the cage identifying them simply as "sisters." Graves tours the three remaining aisles to determine that Willy has not been moved, and then, dazed, he begins by taking out another new arrival, willing himself to hope that his missing companion has gone to a good home. Returning and encountering Peg outside on her break, he asks about the dog who has been in W-12.

He watches closely as she recollects, then feels his fear of the worst confirmed in the look she gives him.

Graves hears the syllables "Oh no" escape him, as if from someone else. Unable to speak further, he feels the color draining from his face.

"Charlie, I'm sorry," she offers, then lays a hand on his wrist. "He had the croup, you know, and you were the only one to give him the time of day," she adds, as if to console.

Graves takes out two more dogs that morning, and after that he does not return.

Most of the time one sees perfectly normal men and women passing by the Station House: just now, for instance, a young man with a cheerful and good-natured face, stepping purposefully toward his place of employment. And here is Graves, just now entering to claim his stool by the window there, where he deposits his book and his jacket. He goes for his coffee and exchanges a greeting with the counterman—no longer Chad, gone further west to new adventure. He opens his book to read while he sips his coffee, then glances up repeatedly, though he could not say, exactly, what it is he hopes to see.

By afternoon, he is raking the first of the leaves to fall in his yard when the high school band begins to practice. While the band plays boldly on the nearby field, Graves retreats the good two miles between his home and the public acres known as Buffalo Park, and there traverses the trail which loops another two miles among the dry grasses and a scattering of ponderosa before a background of more densely forested mountains. The landscape here, affording appealing but not spectacular perspectives, has always pleased him, but he is surprised to find near the end of the loop that a house has been built where it should not have been. Large and manor-like, it has a pitched slate roof that reminds him of the closed-up church downtown, while from behind scrub oak and pine needles it only partially displays its rather gothic countenance. Constructed in his absence, Graves reflects, during the six months he has been distracted by the pound, and probably requiring a special access road, unobservable from where he stands, to threaten thus the sanctity of the park—an encroachment which, though vaguely disturbing to him, seems not altogether incongruent.

A little further on the trail, he finds solace in a more familiar landmark.

A weathered ponderosa, bare and bereft, dead to the world and yet somehow a living presence, stands in a clearing apart from its fellows. Its towering trunk, an almost perfect spire, is only half exposed to the late afternoon sunlight. Graves sits awhile in contemplation, and as the October day deepens the light on the great ruined tree is imperceptibly displaced by shadow.

When he gets back home it is almost dark, and Graves looks up at the autumnal sky where the first of the soundless planets has begun to glow. The silence is almost eerie, yet not for Graves, whose attention is just then given to something none but he can discern. The band has long since dispersed, and no, it is not some phantom remnant of it now distracting him, but rather the faintest of disparate barking, coming not from the neighborhood, he knows, but from further away than a man should be able to detect—from the hills on the far side of the city, if he's not mistaken, from the animal shelter shrouded in the darkening woods. If he concentrates, as he cannot help doing, there rises in his mind a chaotic din, at the same time barely audible, but gathering itself for an ending in a melancholy howl. He fears they will be with him always, these auditory gleanings—though of this, of course, he cannot be sure.

The Westward Inn

When first I discovered it I could not be sure it was real, and then years passed before I could find it again. For the Westward Inn was not to be found waiting beside the exit ramp of any freeway. More residential in nature, it was tucked away in one of the outermost of Southwest City's north-side suburbs, themselves so new and similar as to seem in some inexplicable sense unreal. Further, though the address on Greenhaven Boulevard which I later acquired placed it officially on a main thoroughfare, it was set well back from the street, behind a bank and a new-car dealership. In addition, it was screened from this considerable commerce by a high hedge of oleander which separated its own parking lot from that of the bank and obscured the better part of the sign intended to announce its whereabouts. Thus, in daylight hours, before the neon borders of this reticent landmark could be triggered by darkness, a weary traveler might well pass by on the boulevard and remain oblivious to the Inn.

Nor was it to be found in the telephone book—it had no need to be, as I eventually came to understand. And finally, I could obtain no satisfaction by consulting the directory of Westward Inns, which for reasons none could explain, omitted the one I sought, even though that was its name, the Westward Inn, its outside sign with the emblematic setting sun being in full resemblance with the signs of all those associated inns set down within the pages of this annual guidebook.

Such independence I came to attribute to the character of its owner-managers, Todd and Gloria Wolfenden, whose business card, complete with an address and phone number beneath the name of their establishment, I was careful to file away when I had finally stumbled upon the place again. When on this second visit I made bold to inquire of Gloria about these remarkable circumstances, she dismissed my question with a prompt and slightly embarrassed wave of her hand, offering evasively, "That's a long story." Then she stiffened a bit, perhaps remembering her pride, and added, "Who needs 'em?"

Although I supposed I would never have the details of her long story, I later learned that their refusal to provide nonsmoking rooms had been in part the cause of a drawn out confrontation, for if Gloria and Todd had themselves never formed the habit of smoking, then be it recorded that they were in general a tolerant couple, in this respect like their guests, and bore no malice toward those who had. Whatever the case, if the great chain of Westward Inns had determined to exclude this particular site, then the feeling was mutual, and if some protracted legal contest had transpired, perhaps rendering the new owners unable to list their telephone number, there was nonetheless the fact that their outside sign remained standing, its gold and vermillion—by night, at least—as brave as a banner, suggesting that the Wolfendens, for all their want of artifice, had in the end held their own.

Except for its outside signpost, I used to believe that the Westward Inn was like no other inn. I may as well begin with the matter of its rates, which were surprisingly reasonable. Indeed, one could say with certainty that they were at least a decade behind the times. Even today, when the New Year finds Southwest City glutted with fugitives from the Midwest winter and its hospitality industry is busy making its killing—even in this boom season, the rock-bottom rates of the Inn remained unchanged.

"We've always felt that the average couple deserves a break, too," Gloria Wolfenden has been known to explain, to which the eyes of many an average-income Midwestern couple have been known to grow moist with gratitude. And most such patrons of the Inn were not only middle-income but, like me, well along in late middle age. Some, though, were just young enough to have in their company an elderly parent in his or her dotage, whose barely active life, one speculated, had been prolonged a few years by these merciful winters in the sun.

Quite unaccountably for many onlookers, given the charitable rates which it held to, the Inn was never overrun, not even in winter, when the pressure on the city's lodging capacity swelled to the limit of endurance. To the contrary, its one hundred rooms seemed to be spoken for slowly but surely regardless of the season, filling up nicely at each day's end, and yet seldom, if ever, did an applicant need to be turned away.

To be sure, I often pondered this situation myself, while noticing that year around one could count on a place to stay there simply by arriving during daylight hours—reservations being hardly necessary and even discouraged by the candid owner-managers, the Wolfendens. For most, if not all, of their guests did in fact arrive well before nightfall, sparing their fellow occupants— and themselves as well, one might add—those nocturnal disturbances which invariably accompany the late night check-ins of a certain inconsiderate clientele. Moreover, the Inn's reputation for catering to the elderly, who are even today provided with a discount against the already reasonable rates, served incidentally to hold in check the shouting and running, the raucous music and boisterous merrymaking to be associated with a younger brand of patronage, for the guests of the Inn had not the excess energy, let alone the inclination, for senseless shouting, and most could not have run to save themselves. Kindly old geezers and dowagers, and mild-mannered, middle-aged couples, leavened with a few older traveling men like myself—these, then, were your typical patrons of the Westward Inn.

In view of the foregoing you may have been led to suspect that the steady and felicitous balances between supply and demand at the Westward Inn was owing to some defect in its appearance or some shortcoming in the comfort and cleanliness of the accommodations. If so, then you may rest assured at once that any such suspicion would be false.

It was true that this particular Inn, unlike its former counterparts, could not boast of inside hallways, and it had also to be admitted that despite its many conveniences it did not come equipped with a restaurant on the immediate premises. Yet the regular guests seemed to experience no difficulty in adapting to either of these situations, for not many paces west of the Inn, beyond a kind of service driveway and through a neglected corridor which beckoned from the rear of a rambling slump block structure, you could gain the sidewalk of a busting little mall, and there promenade before a variety of shops and eating establishments—my own predilection, I might here insert, was for the down-home cooking of Blanche at Blanche and Manny's Cafe. And as for the absence of inside hallways, it was quickly to be discerned that such an arrangement would have proven wholly superfluous in the mild winter climate of Southwest City—that the outside ramps were even to be preferred inasmuch as they provided access to that much more of the sunshine which so cheered the hearts of its visitors.

The modest two-story building, laid out in the serviceable shape of an "L," was painted an unblemished white, complemented by rows of forest green doors and shutters, the latter framing the ample latticed windows, and all of which further enhanced the cheerful aspect of the Inn. Inside, under the leadership of Esmeralda, the senior housekeeper, the rooms were kept fresh and immaculate by the staff of six maids whose alacrity at their tasks declared their devotion to the good name of the Inn and the wellbeing of its guests. Outside, the grounds were combed meticulously by the indefatigable Todd Wolfenden and his single helper, a maintenance man by name of Alberto, who would sometimes double as the night front-desk clerk—though the duties of this position, as already implied, could hardly have been termed demanding.

Somehow, Todd always found time to pause in his labors and extend a friendly greeting, such as "How ya doin' today?" Resting a moment on his rake, with his grinning face shaded by his baseball cap and his stalwart sexagenarian frame draped casually in T-shirt and bib overalls, he resembled a Midwestern farmer, which once, if we count the years on the truck farm outside of Des Moines when he was still too young for World War II, he in truth was.

Though not extensive, the carefully tended grounds of the Inn were also thoughtfully planned. To begin, the patrons of the Inn did not step forth from their rooms to confront that all too common eyesore of affordable inns for the middle class, the oppressive terrain of an asphalt parking lot with its grotesque collection of cars, trucks, motor homes, and unsightly grease and oil stains. No, here the guests were faced with an encompassing thicket of desert flora which served as home to an assortment of sparrows and songbirds, including a histrionic mockingbird, not to mention the rarely glimpsed but often heard hummingbirds which were attracted to the several feeders set out by an admiring Gloria Wolfenden. Here flowering ocotillo and mimosa mingled among picturesque saguaro, palo verde, ironwood and date palm trees, and combined with the ground-covering poppies and verbena to form a slender but effective shield. And if one could occasionally detect a patch of bare ground, as along the short flagstone walkways which allowed passage through this miniature bosque, then be it said that the sandy gravel therein was always pleasingly raked and free from the slightest trace of litter, thanks to the vigilance of Gloria's husband Todd.

There was in circulation a story, probably true, that the two of them had not had a vacation together since they had purchased the Inn. Yet it was not likely they gave the matter much thought, since it was obvious that for them fulfillment consisted in seeing to the contentment of their guests, who, upon opening their doors and windows, were afforded the loveliest of prospects, and the pleasures of an enveloping garden with its perennial issue of blossom and birdsong.

It must be admitted, of course, that this slight but highly suggestive embrace of the natural world gave way soon enough to the inevitable man-made parking lot and its contents. And yet, owing to the perseverance of the Wolfendens and the uncanny ministrations of the maintenance man Alberto, the lot of the Westward Inn, situated in the shelter of its "L," was unrepulsive and in its way almost becoming.

For one thing, the extent of this lot was no greater than it needed to be, and like the rooms of the Inn it seemed to fill up snugly, saving just a convenient space or two for that final traveler who would arrive in the twilight. Moreover, there was the welcome green backdrop of the oleander hedge, and its potential wasteland effect was further diminished by the presence in its midst of an island of additional verdure, which until the year twelve B.B.—this abbreviation to be explained in due course—had been the site of the swimming pool. But the new owners at length perceived the latter to be a useless accoutrement in view of the habits of the guests they seemed to be attracting. While thus converting this tract to a more suitable garden spot, on the advice of Alberto they extended its curbing to form a labyrinth of well planted dividers, thereby providing for the parceling of the parking lot's contents into neat and tidy groupings such as one could observe at the more expensive and exclusive resorts—one or another of which, in this instance, may well have served for Alberto's inspiration.

Helpful, too, was the more or less uniform nature of the contents themselves, for the vehicles one encountered at the Inn were seldom of foreign extraction or overgrown to the dimensions of those entities known as "RV's," but mostly older model Chevrolets and Fords, with an occasional Dodge or Plymouth, or once in awhile an aging Mercury thrown in, always the more practical passenger sedans instead of your sports car varieties, and always in hues more subdued than your flashy reds and teals, but somehow kept running and in good working order.

Added to this happy circumstance was the well preserved state of the Inn's pavement, smooth and unbroken, and bleached clean by abundant sunshine. On this reassuring surface the parking spaces were defined by tasteful white stripes, maintained by Alberto, so that the motorists could maneuver their cars into the attractive little coves which awaited them with the greatest of ease. And if ever an insidious grease spot was descried, it needed only for this same Alberto to attack it at dawn with his ingenious compress—and poof! It had vanished by sundown.

Other innovations at the Inn, in addition to the conversion of the swimming pool and the beautification of the parking lot, reflected the further preferences of the familiar clientele. Thus what was once a weight training room had become a bustling guest laundry—the guests invariably sported fresh, clean clothing—and the forgotten video games area, formerly in a small alcove off the lobby, had been refurbished to serve as a quaint but useful little library. Aside from its pair of easy chairs and brass floor lamps on an oriental rug, it also contained a rack which displayed subscriptions to several of the more popular newspapers and periodicals, including *The Minneapolis Star, Reader's Digest*, and *Popular Mechanics*, the latter being a favorite of Alberto whenever he found himself presiding over the front desk during the night shift.

As for books, one might unshelve many of the old standard authors, such as Mark Twain and Charles Dickens, but also the complete works of Zane Grey, the most popular seemingly *Riders of the Purple Sage*, for according to Gloria Wolfenden the wear and tear on this particular title had twice necessitated its replacement. And thanks to Gloria, herself an avid reader, the monthly arrival of a more current title also enriched the collection, by way of her long-standing membership in the Book-of-the-Month Club. Her husband Todd, though never much of a reader himself, had built up a section on gardening and landscaping, which was to all appearances the consuming passion of his life.

And since serious reading may inadvertently become a lonely

preoccupation, it should be here observed that sometimes a meditative reader, too engrossed in the abundant pages of *David Copperfield* to remark the passing of the bedtime hour, would nevertheless be made wary of the presence of a nocturnal visitor. I refer to none other than Matilda, who was no ghost, but the Wolfendens' amiable black lab, who on such occasions was known to desert her customary station behind the Inn's front desk, to pad slowly and softly across the lobby, all wags and smiles, and settling herself gently at the feet of the bookish scholar, to do what she could to comfort this solitary human personage.

But in this brief survey of the Inn's improvements, I must conclude with a word more about what to my mind was the most fortuitous of these: that island of rock garden, where roses and flowering vinca had supplanted the swimming pool at the hub of the Inn's parking lot. While it was true that this oasis was no longer the scene of that joyous splashing where youngsters, we may guess, once filled the air with their frantic cries of "Marco Polo," it had become, as most concurred, something far more in keeping with the Inn's prevailing ambience, being an idyllic retreat which engendered, in contrast to its former function, serenity and calm. For a murmuring fountain, shaded from the noontide heat by four stately poplars, had been provided for its centerpiece, and here many an oldster, collapsed upon the wrought iron bench which adorned the small brickwork terrace, or deposited hither in his or her own wheelchair, was able to while away untroubled hours within the spell of this enchanting device.

And who could judge whether the reveries thus induced in this golden hour were not more blissful, more transporting than the wild enjoyments of the rowdy youth who once frolicked at the site? Certain it was, at any rate, that they were the solace of the nodding gray heads which dreamed there now, there where the trickling overflow fed a little pond of water lilies and, by means of a hidden pump installed and maintained by the wily Alberto, circulated through a meandering rivulet to its source again. And thus was the fountain, unobtrusive and yet wondrous, continuously replenished.

Concerning the person of the maintenance man Alberto, it may now be time to touch upon his origins and character, which for many habitués of the Westward Inn was always something of an enigma and the subject of no little private discussion.

"That's a lot of bunk," Gloria Wolfenden had been known to respond in reference to the rumors which circulated about the owners' coveted handyman. "That man was dying when he showed up here." And it was probably true, as one line of thought had it, that he was a victim of asthma, or some such pulmonary consumption, when he landed on their doorstep in those first years of their tenure. A sailor of Portuguese descent who had toiled most of his life in the North Atlantic fisheries, he fled all the way from Providence, the story went, on some excellent medical advice, for here in the dry desert air, and supported by the tender concern of the Wolfendens, who housed and later employed him, he not only recovered but flourished, proving himself the durable worker we all witnessed, while exhibiting an improbable genius for the mechanical arts as well.

Still, as hinted, all of this was a speculation not uncontested, and there were those who would suggest that the man was little more than an imposter from the city's seedy south side who had been quick to take advantage upon detecting an unsuspecting nature—or in this case a pair of them, for as everyone knew by then Todd Wolfenden was even less circumspect than his wife Gloria. Indeed, it was the absence of any such trait in the proprietors which led most of us to discount the added conjecture that our subject had strayed in from even farther south and that the Wolfendens were harboring a wetback because they knew a good thing when they saw it.

Still other inventions, some of which would seem to plead for the maintenance man's immediate dismissal, had achieved the proportions of the outlandish—inventions, for example, which imputed to him an expertise in firearms as well as other forms of mayhem, and which purported that he was nothing less than the foothold in Southwest City for the New York Mafia.

And although it may have been true, as some insisted, that the previously cited compresses for removing the parking lot blemishes were concocted largely with gunpowder, I had it on authority from a knowledgeable housewife that the basis of these compounds was nothing other than ordinary baking soda. And this same good woman, incidentally, would explain that Alberto's flair for things mechanical was merely the odds and ends of information acquired by constantly boning up on *Popular Mechanics*.

These sundry disparagements were sadly intensified during that relatively brief interval marked by the visit of Alberto's brother—or such, at least, was our assumption about the stranger who for the weeks in question shared his dwelling place, the room upstairs in the back with the long view toward the city's south side. But enough for the moment, unless the impression be conveyed that among those for whom he so faithfully and courteously discharged his duties the former seafaring man was the object of a universal and hostile mistrust, for such was in no way the case. Even today, as we observe this same humble Alberto going steadily about his routine, his shoulders now slightly stooped with age and his glossy, almost comical mustache the only salient feature on the face in the shadow of his clean white pith helmet, we are struck with shame, surely, at the mention of these persistent innuendos, and as we examine our hearts for what could be the true assessment of our attitude toward the unassuming maintenance man, I venture to conclude that the great majority of us here at the Inn discover only affection.

At the blind east end of the Westward Inn, at the top of the "L," a break in its enclosing thicket permitted space for a shuffleboard court, horseshoe pits, and a satellite dish, the latter being a state-of-the-art accomplishment by none other than this same Alberto, and each revealing how the guests of the Inn availed themselves of additional amusements, all more social in nature than the solitary distractions of reading.

Of these, predictably, watching television was the most popular. And yet here again the characteristic taste of the viewers had resulted in a curious circumstance, so that strolling by the rooms where the green doors sat amicably ajar of a sunny afternoon or a warm evening, and thus gleaning a sampling of the programs in progress, one necessarily forsook the present for what was visibly a kindlier past. For in general the guests had little use for depictions of violence and vice, and having no conscious needs to gratify morbid or paranoid tendencies and forty-two channels to select from, they inclined toward a sunnier bill of fare, the staples of which were old re-runs of such shows as "Gomer Pyle," "Gilligan's Island," and "Beverly Hillbillies," where good-natured, likable protagonists inspired an amiable and trusting disposition.

Such disposition may well have been a motivating factor among those who, on Sunday mornings, took temporary leave of the Inn in order to attend the church of their choice. I sometimes pondered whether there was a difference during the remainder of the week between those who did and those who did not, but I could come to no definite conclusions, and simply note that the contingent which undertook this weekly outing did not include the Wolfendens, although for the convenience of the guests, and perhaps as an encouragement for them to exercise this fundamental right, they did keep a directory of churches posted in the lobby.

I could never locate any churches in the immediate vicinity, but Sunday morning was surely one occasion when the guests did not mind getting dressed up and taking short excursions in their cars—which, as already remarked, were reliable but could hardly have been deemed luxurious. Similarly, getting dressed up did not entail putting on anything expensive or ostentatious, but rather garments which, though clean and neatly pressed, were obviously the attire of former working men and women, the accessories of which did not include, for example, the white, shiny, plastic-looking belts and shoes for men so often encountered at the aforementioned exclusive Southwestern resorts. In short, there was much about the patrons of the Inn to suggest that a sizable number of them, indeed, may well have been Democrats, and I shall long recall the evening I was passing through the parking lot when my head was turned by what appeared to be, on the bumper of a worn Chevy Malibu from South Dakota, a slogan of some sort. I paused, and upon closer inspection of this rarity for the cars at the Inn, realized I was standing face to face with the fading remains of an old McGovern sticker.

Although I did not discover any cliques among those who frequented the Inn, they did tend to form friendships and often fell into the habit of keeping each other company. Thus, of a Sunday morning, it would not have been remarkable to behold piling into some faithfully waiting sedan not just its owners but a happy foursome in bright anticipation of the sermon by, say, the Reverend Rumford at The Good Shepherd, to be followed by dinner at, say, Sir Cedric's, or some other popular buffet-style restaurant. Moreover, if you happened to pass by a half-open door at the Inn that same afternoon, it would hardly have been out of the ordinary to spy not only the occupants but another couple as well, residents of some other room, engaging in some pleasant badinage while watching a rerun of "I Love Lucy."

For in a sense, it must be allowed, the generation at the Inn were all "re-running," which they unequivocally preferred to keeping up with the times, so to speak. But, if running or some such frenetic pastime was your pleasure, then you had only to climb the stairway at the crook of the "L" for the view from the second-story breezeway. Here the land behind the Inn fell gradually away, and here at sundown I was soon to behold, along with the sprawling and seemingly endless environs of Southwest City as it faded away into the glowing dusk, the surprising proximity of that city's Greyhound Park. It was far enough removed to be out of earshot, its spacious parking lot buffering the Inn from its stadium, and yet within walking distance, a pleasant hike, for from below me came the sound of voices in soft conversation, punctuated here and there with a chuckle and a little swell of mirth. Peering down, I detected a number of my fellow guests, in little groups of four or six, wending their way homeward along the oleander-bordered path which connected the Inn's backside with the racetrack parking area. The lot was almost empty at that moment, the afternoon's races being concluded. Probably, I considered, it was just such over-the-hill fans as these who kept this obsolescent sport alive, and I vowed that in the future I would join them.

And standing there alone against a serene and monumental sunset, I experienced a rare moment of insight in which I saw how the Wolfendens, in their dedication to their humane enterprise, had created not only a working place which insured the survival of six industrious maids and a rejuvenated Alberto, but a refuge for innumerable weary pilgrims who were permitted such consolations as I, though a passive bystander, could in that moment sense pervading my entire being: such warmth, such cheer, such human fellowship.

Such relationships at the Westward Inn, however, were necessarily shifting and tentative, given the mature age of the average guest and the normal limitations of the human life span, and also taking into account the ill health which was often a factor in swaying its victims to the region in the first place. But to this I should add that here, as elsewhere, one also chanced upon mere human fallibility and inconstancy, and an instance which touches upon my own experience may serve to illustrate all that has been here expounded.

In the course of their migrations to the Inn Ben and Myrnadean Littlefield of St. Paul, Minnesota, became fast friends with the MacGruders, Hank and Camille, of Fort Dodge, Iowa. I myself formed an acquaintance with Ben and Myrnadean one evening when I accepted their invitation to join them at their table in Blanche and Manny's place, the available tables being scarce on that particular evening. I should here explain that Ben Littlefield, as well as I could observe, was a man esteemed by many about the Inn, not excluding the Wolfendens' black lab Matilda, by whom he was often sought out and nuzzled, and whom he was fond of petting. A retired librarian of frail constitution, he never failed to express a genuine interest in whatever one tried to tell him. Respect accrued to him also, no doubt, because of his wife, Myrnadean. No longer youthful, of course, she yet retained a delicate beauty, especially about the eyes, I thought, where a soft-spoken wisdom seemed to reside. In short, they made me feel at home in their company, and yet when, that weekend, I tagged along with them and the MacGruders to our nearby Greyhound Park, I realized of a sudden that I was now a participant in that very fellowship which I had previously savored at a safe remove, and I confess that the experience proved in some obscure way a disappointment—as though the thing itself had fallen short of my imagining of it.

Later that evening, while the five of us were watching a re-run of "Gunsmoke" in Hank and Camille's place, I tried to shed my melancholy and made what proved to be a sadly inept attempt to join the party. It was during a break in the action that Hank rose from his armchair to offer us a challenge.

"Betcha none of y'all—'ceptin' Camille here, of course—know where I was born was the same place as Festus." He paused to grin. "Know where that was?"

On one of the many highways I'd travelled around the Mountain West for my living, there was a sign I had often passed at the edge of the town in question. I saw my chance and blurted the answer.

"Las Animas, Colorado. Birthplace of Curtis Gates."

Silence. Poor Hank's jaw was drooping.

"You know that, do you?"

"And just up the river, at La Junta, there's the ruins of Bent's Old Fort," I offered, struggling to get beyond my gaffe.

"Be durn'd if he don't know that, too," Hank stammered.

I had intended to proceed by asking what he knew about the road that led south out of La Junta, but I glimpsed his hurt, and suddenly realizing that what I knew was not one jot of what I didn't, I decided to let it go at that.

Whatever the case, our companionship was destined to be brief. Upon checking in for my week in January the following year, I soon confronted, to my dismay, an obituary, clipped from the *Star* and pinned to the Inn's bulletin board, announcing the demise of Ben Littlefield, who had succumbed to pneumonia in the onset of the Minnesota winter. I harbored a vague notion that Myrnadean, at least, might yet be arriving in the company of the MacGruders, but this hope was soon enough dashed when I overheard a rumor making the rounds. Back in Fort Dodge, it seemed, in favor of a younger man—and, I found myself assuming, a man less gruff and more polished—Camille MacGruder had divorced her husband Hank. And her husband Hank, shy and uncertain, I'd sensed, beneath his crusty exterior, had not the wherewithal to bring himself again to the Inn, let alone Myrnadean.

That January, as the old familiar faces were showing up at the Inn, I strolled alone and missed the ones I had most looked forward to seeing, while the black retriever Matilda, herself looking old and enfeebled, wandered forlornly among the arriving guests and vainly sought her favorite. Like the spots and stains beneath the miraculous compounds of Alberto, the good man seemed to have vanished with a "poof."

Concerning Alberto's wonderful parking lot spot remover, there remains yet another opinion which must now be alluded to. At the same time I must now attempt to enlarge upon the man we identified as Alberto's brother, since it was he who under considerable duress advanced it.

Given a certain light, it is true that he bore his brother a certain resemblance. Or, given a certain frame of mind induced by the wild surmisings he ignited about the two of them, he became, as it were, his brother's darker self. A younger, somewhat swarthier and obviously less disciplined sibling, he skulked about with a sour impatience, as though unable to discover any detail about the milieu of the Inn which was not distasteful to him. Esmeralda, the senior housekeeper, denounced him for his "evil eye," while Matilda uncharacteristically whined and sought a retreat from his presence, which daily became less welcome. For almost the length of his stay his thin, clenched lips bespoke contempt without ever uttering a sound.

In fairness, and just as some of us suspected, it should be allowed that his taciturnity was at least in part to be attributed to a language barrier, for at last I overheard him, in the lobby before the Wolfendens, endeavoring mightily but haltingly to express himself, as though unable to further suppress the pent up feeling with which he groped for the words so obviously foreign to him.

"Go on, get outta here," was all he got for his trouble, for such was the bluff response of Gloria Wolfenden, it being apparent that in spite of his fulminations she could not take the man seriously. More to the point, perhaps, was the likelihood that neither she nor her husband Todd could appreciate the ramifications of the argument placed before them, the essentials of which were these: notwithstanding the marvelous efficiency of Alberto's concoction—which the speaker had witnessed his brother, on hands and knees, applying that very morning—and regardless of what might be the elusive ingredients therein, it was a remedy which he insisted should never have been brought to bear in the first place, for in his view of the matter the parking lot stains demanded no remedy and needed only to be left in peace.

"Keep these spots! These spots they are good!" he raged at the end, by which I inferred, with the help of his waving hands, he meant good for the guests. Yet he must have despaired of making his audience comprehend, for even as I grasped at his meaning—experienced just an inkling of the depths it touched upon—he ceased his gesticulations and, in the wake of Gloria's succinct dismissal, abruptly made his exit.

Later, returning to my room that evening, I saw him packing the trunk of his red Ferrari, and as I passed close by we both were suddenly made spectators to an occurrence which must have been unprecedented within the bounds of the Inn. Three skateboarding youths, their caps turned backwards, came slashing through the parking lot, then had the temerity to ascend the stairs at the bottom of the "L" and go rolling along the second-story ramp, yelling all the while. By the time an alerted Todd Wolfenden could give them chase they were down the far stairwell and making away, leaving the befuddled proprietor to ponder the abuse they bequeathed him on quavering voices, and the unmistaken obscene gesture which the uplifted hand of the smallest had flaunted.

Turning to the Ferrari, I found myself admiring the transformation taking place on the countenance of its owner. The long thin lips unclenched, and in that single instance I beheld them curled in a satisfied smile. He started his car, and perhaps taking to heart the impromptu advice extended earlier by the Inn's proprietress, he did indeed get out of there.

The departure of Alberto's brother—assuming we did not arrive at this relationship in error—was accompanied by a general sigh of relief, and yet a certain tension lingered, something new and disturbing to the Westward Inn, so that I for one began to fear that the relaxed and friendly spirit which once prevailed there was never to be recovered. An incident pertaining to the Inn's proprietor confirmed my uneasiness and may serve to illustrate the transformation to which I was unwillingly attuned.

It happened that the omission of a restaurant from the Inn itself would now and then produce audible misgivings, albeit these came primarily from newcomers rather than established patrons, and it was the custom of the owners to endure these expressions of mild dissatisfaction without taking noticeable umbrage. Yet such expressions may well have been the source of some sore spot lurking beneath the natural good humor of Todd Wolfenden, for during the interval I speak of a complaint addressed one evening to the Inn's proprietress moved him to suddenly intervene and to deliver a most uncharacteristic response. Since I was in the library at the time and thus within hearing, I won't forget his surprising ferocity.

"Whatch ya think this place is, Mac?" he exploded. "Better git on down to the Holiday Inn! We can't help ya here!" And thus in the grip of his wrath he drove the prospective guest from the premises, only to then turn sheepishly to his abashed wife Gloria in order to confide his wish that they had bought a farm instead. "I just like being around animals and stuff," he added meekly, by way of a limp but somehow touching explanation.

Such outbursts as this were not uncommon in the wake of the brother's departure. Though the term of his stay was scarcely more than a fortnight, it proved an undeniable turning point in the annals of the Inn, so that in listening to one guest reminisce with another, one acquires familiarity with the expressions "B.B" and "A.B.," for just as the day may be divided into its A.M. and P.M. hours, so the era of the Westward Inn has found its natural meridian in the brief but ominous visitation of the dissenting outsider whom some would brand a malevolent devil. Thus the designation "Before" or "After the Brother" conjures up for those who employ it the demarcation of many subtle distinctions pertaining to the Inn. Chief among these, and perhaps a key to the inscrutable heart of the matter, must surely be that the wholesome, spontaneous laughter and chuckles which one used to savor there have given way to a laughter which is at best controlled, considered, and almost hesitant.

But to avail myself of this usage, it was still within the first year A.B., on a Saturday at the neighboring mall, that I underwent a singular encounter, and though you may call it trivial compared with the mute admonitions of Alberto's brother, it yet played a part to further my reflections.

Puffed up with a satisfying lunch at Blanche's, and dallying a moment on the sidewalk there, I noticed I had caught the eye of a youth who was even then advancing in my direction. It was not surprising that he singled me out, for the pedestrian traffic on our stretch of the walk had fallen strangely calm, and I won't deny that there was something extraordinary about that moment. I had a premonition I was about to be rudely accosted by one of the erstwhile skateboarders I had witnessed invading the Inn, and perhaps, given this youth's small stature, the very one who had signaled their harsh defiance on taking their leave. But the voice I heard addressing me was gentle and subdued with courtesy.

"Pardon me, sir. Do you have the time?"

Except for his polite "Thank you" when I had glanced at my watch and told him it was half past noon, this was the sum of our exchange. Turning, he moved slowly away, and I spent the remainder of the day recalling how lost and alone he had seemed, how much in need of befriending. Yes, I'd gladly complied with his simple request, but even in that slight gesture I may have done him no favor, for on my return to the Inn I discovered, along with the stirrings of a vague regret, that my watch had stopped.

As for me, I prefer to think I harbor no hard feelings toward Alberto's brother, for the changes he must have foreseen seem now ineluctable. I can see by their eyes that the other guests, too, are aware that the times are changing. They belong to a disappearing class and generation, and despite their Heartland heritage their hearts are rooted with fear of the world's end. The oleander hedges will not stop the bullets of drive-by shootings, brought home to us by an incident behind the nearby Greyhound Stadium, and loud rap from the boulevard interrupts the meditations by the fountain. The gardens are fouled with unraked litter, and already, at the end of a decade A.B., the parking lot stains have gone for years untreated, for he who once attended to them must now conserve his waning energies, once thought to be boundless, for his nocturnal duties as patrolling watchman.

The green doors of the Inn can no longer be left invitingly ajar, and companions are hard to come by. And now, in the still of the nights we used to think would be forever tranquil, the door to the Wolfendens' quarters may sometimes be heard to slam, yet it fails to conceal the exchanges which follow, heated, accusatory, profane. They grow old and vituperative, and as everyone now understands, their Westward Inn will one day be reduced to a tenement hovel no different from those on the city's south side, and already the south sides of cities begin to multiply.

"So this is what it has come to," I find myself thinking—all the generations, and my own youth, too, and the exuberance, subdued but true, that came with westering.

As for me again, I hold on tight to the Inn of the days gone by, though it be but the fluff of a dream. Waking in the mornings, I crack my window to admit the sound of voices rising from the entrance drive below, and for just a moment's reprieve I'm certain that I recognize my friends returning, but when I look I find that I'm mistaken. I wander the grounds by day, and often I stroll the boulevard and the adjacent mall. By evening, it seems, I'm always crossing the parking lot, and then, pausing there among the multitude of blemishes, remarking to myself how old I am, and how alone, I dwell upon that sea of stains until I'm gone.

The Roads Around Perdido

I

You'll like, first of all, the way the road gets you out of town. Don't ask me how I know. Trust me. Find a car, if you can, that doesn't guzzle fuel. Keep to the old road north of the river. You'll like the way it winds easily along and has you among fields and cottonwoods in the time it takes you to discover that your heart is singing.

At the ruins of the old fort, where the road crosses the river and joins the U.S. Highway, you cross too, but then keep south instead, following the back road. Well beyond the town you'll come to a place where the sky has opened, light-stricken now. Once you lose it, you've heard them say, you can never get it back. It is early morning in the middle of May and the earth is green and grassy smelling. The ditches run full of water, and by the roadside you can see the grass grows dense and rich, vermillion-tipped, wind-rippled into gentle waves.

Untended fields give way to unplanted prairie, and then through hills of juniper and sky the highway dips and rises, a slate-bright line to the end of the earth where clouds, new-born and luminous, have just begun to billow. The world, thus green, then white, then blue, is all infused with light until you scarcely believe in me, all momentarily so right you'll find a cry of heaven rising to your lips, expending itself in silence.

Silence, you've heard them say, is golden. I could tell you where you're going, but I won't. I watch you come upon a tributary of the river, sense your solace in the few green fields surviving close beside it, and then you wind and climb among the juniper again, a view opening up behind you, until the land begins to level and you feel the long unlikely arm of these High Plains beneath you, grasslands wild and sun-seared, with wildflowers blowing in the wind.

Toward morning's end a great but gentle dog appears by the roadside. Old and lost, as you can see, he makes a mute appeal for you to take him in. You hesitate. They told you every boy should have one, and you did. He looks at you as if he knows you. They say it's who you know, not what, but you know no one. You hesitate, and then you drive on by.

Afternoon will find you at a pass among low-lying mountains, a pass that's hard to find and little known, but known to you. There's the village sleeping there without a soul in sight, now as then. Yes, you say some memory begins to stir? Once you've known it, do you ever lose it altogether? Some other day in spring, in another year, you passed this way from the other side. From the sun-swept sky a sprinkling of rain was falling, and you stopped in this village which you took to be deserted, got out and walked around the streets here with your heart struck full of wonder. You sought and found a general store, went in, and stood around convinced no one was there. Turning to leave, you heard a door ease open and the floor begin to creak, and there beside the counter a man in a white apron appeared, inquisitive. You told him what you were looking for.

"Well, stick your head in there," he growled, and swung open the door of a great glass cooler, half empty but surprisingly deep.

You did, and found what you were seeking, whereupon the man relented with a smile. And on you traveled, quenching your thirst, wondering still.

The pass you cross seems never steep but long in its descent through sloping pastures, boulder-strewn and edged with sparse and silent stands of scanty timber. Silence may be golden, as they say, but I speak to you with my silence. Through these you pass, and then at last you are there, in a lonely country of stunted, wind-riven buttes and mountains, of mesas stacked on tilting mesas till beyond your vision, where thunder sounded as the pavement turned to dust and then to slippery mud when the rain began to fall, and in what seems now another life you watched the antelope go bounding single file down the edge of the beveled earth. Look for me in the crumbling hamlets set far apart, in the homesteads fallen open to the sky. You've heard them say we'll always have the poor among us, but here, when darkness gathers you'll begin to sense my presence. You are here in the place where I am waiting for you.

You are here, lost in your dream of another river and the town somewhere beyond it, a town called Perdido with an inn where once you paused for awhile, weary from travel. You saw the upstairs windows facing out on a pleasant plaza, but you were shown instead to a room which looked down an alley toward a mountain off in the distance, different from all the others, standing there alone in the fading light. In the spring evening snow began to fall, causing you worry at first, but then kept falling as you sat by the sill of your half-open window, obliterating all, until you fell asleep in your chair and awoke renewed in the brilliant morning. Off in the distance, you could see that the mountain was gone.

II

No, you never set your foot upon it, but on and on you lingered. Weeks, months went by.

Sierra Escondida, you heard it called by those taciturn few old timers willing to acknowledge its reality, one of whom was witness to your faux pas, your sudden consternation when, on that morning as you attempted to draw him out, you broached the subject of the Sierra Encantada. Your acquaintance stared at you blankly, his deeply tanned and creased face seeming to slacken, but finding yourself unable or unwilling to explain, you let the conversation drop. For in that moment you had glimpsed some undiscovered spectrum to your life, clearing your vision of doubt and overcast, and you understood that the Sierra Encantada, having attained by a slip of the tongue its proper calling, had thus been summoned to its true existence.

"The further away the better it looks," you heard it put by one of your acquaintances, to the less than heartfelt amusement of all those present at the time, but it was true, as you learned soon enough, that mere proximity had little or no effect upon your ability to comprehend the Sierra.

You strolled one morning to the southern edge of town, where people lived in squalor, and found your mountain sunken from your view. On the other hand, you spent the better part of another day wandering northerly, while the Sierra stood firm. All the same, whenever you attempted to study it for any duration, to examine it in detail, it had a way of letting you know you could not be sure just what you were looking at, and such times as these you wished you might draw nearer to it. Days you wasted in your attempts to do just that, only to discover in the end that you were as far removed from it as before. It was an old deception, of course, of mountains and deserts, so that even while wondering whether some other course should not be taken, you once determined to push forward, trusting to reason that the distance between yourself and the object of your fascination must be gradually diminishing, all the while endeavoring to keep that object in sight—except, of necessity, when you were forced to descend into an arroyo or to negotiate an abutment of boulders or similar natural obstructions.

And at last, indeed, you did come face to face with a mountain—or rather, face to feet, finding yourself positioned down below it—and yet only to doubt, to suspect that this was not it at all, not the one, not what you had seen from the distance nor what you had all along had in mind. And at just such times you questioned all over again its very existence—just as, from time to time, you wonder still about your own.

You could never discredit, by means of your own investigations, the persistent belief that there were no roads into the Sierra. From time to time you heard mention of "the old road" which may once have skirted its eastern flank while delivering an intermittent trickle of settlers in another century, and although it was allowed that traces of this old highway were still to be found, you could never attest to having come across these in person. Neither, apparently, were there any substantial watersheds which might have enticed surveyors and cartographers to trace them to their sources, a phenomenon less surprising when you considered the arid surroundings from which the Sierra rose. And while it was known that the pale green lacings throughout its environs suggested a system of springs and occasional parks and meadows, and that the darker greens and blues of its higher elevations, discernable even at considerable distances, could be attributed to a certain extent of timbered forest, it was also true that no mineral wealth had ever been detected there.

And all to the mountain's great good fortune, you could see, for surely it was in part this very paucity of exploitable elements which had allowed the Sierra to pass the years in solitude and peace, sparing it, among other destructions, the debilitating alarms of the bulldozer's back-up signals, along with the frontal assaults of those earth-moving engines which had elsewhere so disfigured the earth they once roamed, shifting it senselessly about. Instead, existing on little and never in need of more, surviving a great depletion and a vast diminishment, the Sierra had endured all the while on that neglected edge of your vision in an unfathomable serenity.

While it was true that the Sierra had big shoulders, steep and forbidding sides, and so far as had been determined, no access roads, it remained a wonder to you that it had never been violated by that determined faction of sportsmen with their ingenious accessories, normally deterred by no obstacle.

The theories were several, as you encountered them, but doubtless the most appealing attributed the absence of all such aggression to the solitude and beauty of the mountain itself, which was deemed capable of penetrating the hardest of hearts and affecting even the least redeemable specimens of human nature. A worthy opinion, surely, and one which harbored the fondest of hopes not only for the future of the Sierra but for that of humanity as well. Yet you yourself were inclined to an explanation far simpler and less optimistic, or as those of you who subscribed to it would have preferred, merely more realistic: the theory, that is, that all who would trespass upon the Sierra Encantada were unable to do so, no, not because of their own incapacity or—still less tenable—some wondrous change from within, but simply because in the last analysis they were unable to violate that which they could not see or comprehend.

It was said that if one waited patiently there would come those few days in the year when thin streaks of gold would make a brief appearance high in the Sierra—the turning leaves of the mountain aspen. But one must watch diligently, you were told, for they seemed always to vanish upon second or third sighting. "Nothing gold can stay," someone said, recalling the words of a poet.

You watched, but could never be certain, and then one morning you awoke in a reverie about a day gone by. You had been dreaming, standing in silence and pondering your great mountain, when something moving darkly like a shadow brushed your neck, stirred the air about your face and then was swiftly gone. You turned in time to glimpse the large, lone scavenger, a member of that usually gregarious species, the black-feathered ravens. You had never been touched by one before, not even while dreaming, nor could you comprehend the meaning of this particular boldness, but you remembered walking early on an autumn morning in the city where you lived, crossing the deserted streets and parking lots, and watching, as you passed, their slow-winged ascent into the clearing sky, touched just then with light, and knowing even then how that morning walk had been by them made memorable.

Although it is true that the Sierra rises from semi-arid surroundings, you were close enough to the Great Divide to be visited by snow storms. Often the snow would descend silently and peacefully, but on occasion it could be accompanied by wind enough to make a blizzard. Yet such storms were inevitably of brief duration, never enduring beyond the day they precipitated, and the snow, dry and powdery to begin with, evaporated by the middle of the day following, save perhaps in those shadowy places having only a northern exposure, where it might cling until replenished by the next snowfall, but on that morning after—always, you could count on it—you were greeted by a blinding sun.

On such occasions, looking southward, you reasoned you might thus expect to find some faint tracing of the powdery substance in the higher elevations of the Sierra, and yet you trained your gaze in that direction only to find all such expectations denied, to find, indeed—what was most remarkable— nothing at all, save for the dry, pure, crystalline air in that brilliant morning light which seemed to extend forever.

"Here today and gone tomorrow," you heard them say, intoned in a manner which suggested a lighter heart than you yourself were able to summon. You sought consolation in the assurances that such a disappearing act could only be explained as an optical illusion, and yet you could not ignore the possibility that the truth resided in the reverse proposition: it was the mountain, some contended, which was the illusion, and not its disappearance.

Still, most of you who had seen the Sierra held steadfast to your belief that it remained somewhere on the southern horizon. You had only to fix your gaze in the right place, at the right moment when the light was not too deceptive, and your faith would surely be rewarded. And indeed, it occurred to you—or rather, it was somewhere suggested and you were readily disposed to accept the notion—that the entire phenomenon was simply one more subterfuge of the Sierra for preserving its wonderful hidden wellsprings and securing its continuity, while further explaining why no discharge from the hunter's rifle had ever been reported there, nor even, so far as was known, the footfall of its first explorer.

On such mornings, when you awoke to find the Sierra no longer there, evaporated with the insubstantial mists of the dawn, or as you preferred to believe, temporarily invisible, the sense of loss was inconsolable, culminating, as the day advanced, if not in utter dejection, in a malaise of spirit from which there was no relief or distraction. The restlessness became unbearable, and if the night were warm and the moon were up you felt compelled to venture out.

Yes, something told you that there must be moonlight. On that last evening at the end of a day in spring when the wind was warming, you made what seemed an endless trek along barely discernable trails through a wilderness of rough and rock-strewn hills, all in the waning moonlight. When at last it had vanished you sat on a stone and rested in the darkness. You dozed into the dawn and awoke just at sunrise to the bark of a dog—a dog on his own in the wilderness, you assumed, his bark a single, drawn-out yowl, pitched high and plaintive, encompassing both pain and joy. Rising in that morning light, you were conscious mainly of the ensuing silence, and then, gradually, of the calling and singing of many birds, their songs barely familiar but never sung so sweetly, whereupon you lifted up your face and surveyed the precarious height of your Sierra Encantada.

Among those who had seen it, it was common knowledge that once you had set your sight upon the Sierra, it would never disappear from your life entirely. To which, upon your leave taking, you were ready to assent, and to which you were also ready to add, following your deliberation that your own experience was probably not in this respect unique, that once you had seen the Sierra Encantada you would soon discover that you lived for nothing else—for no other purpose, that is, than to see it again, and again, and indeed, to exist in its presence for as long and as often as you were able.

III

You are here, in the country where your car starts to sputter and your road begins to end—or rather, ends in a senseless junction with another, in a "T" in the middle of nowhere, atop a high, wide mesa where a sagging wooden house is barely standing, alone against the sunset. In another year, or another life, you were hailed from the yard beyond the peeling picket fence by a burnt-out man with a garden hose, a veteran of the war that was lost half way around the world, patiently watering his thriving weeds as if they were grass. You've heard them telling how the grass gets greener just beyond the hills. They say you live and learn, but then you've noticed that they don't. You pulled up to the old outmoded pump out front for gas and were waited on by a lady, tall and comely, whom you took to be his wife, a lady gentle in her conversation with a great but gentle dog at her side who smiled at you and wagged his tail.

This time, you ease to a stop at the top of the "T," grateful for the worn strip of pavement which awaits you there. The wind has shifted, and it could be a deception of the dying light, but as you make your turn something is moving in the yard beyond the ruined fence—and then you see the lady passing there.

She pauses and turns to look at you. You have just time to lift your arm and wave, to sense her gentleness again as she returns your greeting. Once you lose them, you know by now what happens. But the moment has passed for you to stop. She could not have known you, you are thinking, and you could have only alarmed her by stopping. There is only the mute gesture in the failing light, and slowly gaining speed, you drive on down the weed-choked road that's glowing in the sundown.

They say it's who you know, but don't you believe them. Trust me instead. You know no one, but if I know you—and I do—you'll push on toward the river. Slowly, carefully, you'll descend the grade of its canyon in the darkness, and with your windows down, hear the water lapping, as you cross the narrow little bridge. Half way up the other side your car will sputter again and quit. It will cross your mind that you could walk back—it is not that far—back to the sagging house on the mesa top where the moon is rising and the wind has died, to the lady who lives there alone. "I'll take you in," she would say. And it's true, I should tell you. She'd take you in for the length of an endless night.

Do you know who I am?

Yes, now I think you begin to. And I know you. You could turn back, but you won't. You'll walk on through the night that's lush with your dreaming toward the end you can barely remember, and somewhere well beyond the river you'll come to the little town with the inn and the window where snow begins to fall and in the distance down the alley a mountain comes and goes. You'll enter, too weary to have gone another step, bone-tired and out of gas, as the saying holds, and sitting there safe at last in the place you were looking for, by the sill of your opened window, you'll hope the snow will fall forever.

And it will.

Report on the Hadleyburg Renaissance

"But at last, in the drift of time, Hadleyburg
had the ill luck to offend a passing stranger...."
—Mark Twain, "The Man that Corrupted Hadleyburg"

No one, it seems, can offer a satisfying explanation for the new "phenomena" which are everywhere observable, and a number of these developments, such as the so-called Renaissance at Hadleyburg, have passed without even an adequate recording. Though I make no attempt to account for these anomalies, I date the bulk of them, and certainly my awareness of them, from our celebrated Maladeux case, after the youth who was, to be sure, part anarchist demon, but also, if one cares to be honest about his total legacy in the context of our times, part prophet. Since Maladeux, for instance—and so some take him for the cause—one sees this isolation of our youth, this separation, perhaps unconscious, from what was once the mainstream of our lives. Thus we observe—we live with—the phenomenon of their own music, their own gangs, their own world. And thus we feel the edge of their contempt, or often the duller edge of their profound indifference, manifested from time to time in some spontaneous hostility—all, of course, as Maladeux, in so many words, had prophesied.

True enough, the paper boy still makes his rounds, as far as I can tell unharmed, just after dawn, and the newspapers he delivers are still printed daily, on schedule, as if to belie or somehow dissipate the disquieting effects of their contents—and more on this directly. But well before the paper boy is stirring, when the first prospects of those fine mornings of midsummer entice me up and about, I have heard, coming from around the corner and down the block, the most obscene laughter, aggressive, rude, and, I am sorry to say, youthful, rendering it, for reasons I cannot explain, the more chilling and foreboding.

But to illuminate, hopefully, my references to "the context of our times" and the unsettling contents of our daily papers, I have only to turn to the seemingly endless sources of our anxieties and to focus on one of the more alarming and bewildering of these, which, though for awhile the preoccupation of the entire media, by cautious and tacit agreement now seems happily to have run its course. Yes, I refer to that wave, or rather those drawn out waves in curious succession, of motiveless murders, unpredictable as they were abhorrent, and resulting in a situation which was in a sense paradoxical for our police, who were at once baffled and gratified. Gratified, because after years of trying vainly to convince their critics of the dangers and difficulties of their calling, they were at last witnessing the spectacle of a changing public demeanor, a demeanor formerly arrogant, insouciant or at best merely tolerant, but which soon became something perhaps best described as abject and sycophantic. And with good reason, for as this inscrutable menace extended the reach of its tentacles, it touched the heart, if not the more tangible person, of every law-abiding citizen, so that if one knew not a victim or two personally he at least knew someone who did. I well recall that one appointed official made bold to suggest that this citizenry was reaping its "just desserts," as he put it, a pronouncement surely calculated, one would have thought, to raise a clamor for his removal, and yet the only consequence I ever detected was a proliferation of sulking suspicions that the crimestoppers, far from doing their duty, were content to see the public ordeal prolonged.

And who could deny that the general dismay was augmented by the fact that the vast majority of these crimes remained unsolved? Indeed, has anyone noticed that to date not a single suspect has been brought to trial? But of course, I should not be speaking of "suspects," for there were none. It's true that a few of the cases were dispatched under the heading of "suicide," and the usual number of dubious confessions were received. Yet surely the case for the authorities, on the whole, rested on the most insubstantial footing, for whereas it was easy to allow, as they contended, that their poor record in bringing the perpetrators of these singular deeds to any sort of justice was owing precisely to this same singularity—that is, I mean, to the absence of any motives involved—while this was easy enough to allow, as I was saying, it was at the same time not so easy to overlook their reticence to produce an honest accounting, a sound estimate, as to just how many such perpetrators were the cause of it all. In other words, while assigning responsibility to this or that suicide for the chain reactions which they admitted had claimed dozens of lives, should not the authorities have been speaking instead of homicides, and in terms of hundreds, thousands, yes, perhaps even hundreds of thousands of lives? Finding no discernible pattern to these random slayings, or more accurately, discovering a "multiplicity of patterns"—which rendered their use of the term questionable—they ought to have been the first to suspect and admit to the ever increasing incidence of this unseemly contagion. But no, it remained for the public at large, goaded no doubt by the media, to engage in erratic surmisings, and meanwhile these somber and sometimes grisly acts of gratuitous aggression, thought at first to be the deeds of a remote handful which one merely heard about, so multiplied as to come home to roost in every township throughout the country, spurring yet another migration from rural to urban environments, this time by those who sought the protective shelter of the anonymity afforded by the latter,[1] and sparing none from the necessity of reflecting that he or she was living in a land harboring no mere "handful" of compulsive killers, but what on the contrary must be "many handfuls" of them, for how else was one to account for the epidemic magnitude of this newest and most pressing dilemma among an already debilitating array of social calamities? Still, while pleading the impossibility of their task, the police were quick enough to make a showing of whatever tentative shreds of evidence they could come by, for even though the killings they dealt with seemed senseless they were not, after all, insensible, and this, they were able to grasp, was in back of the unfamiliar attention—in certain quarters, the respect, even—which they felt bestowed upon them, and which, even while baffled, they found finally so gratifying.

But as already touched upon, this strange aberration subsided in its own good time, thanks in part, I like to think, to the ameliorating influence of the unanticipated happening at Hadleyburg, though some dismiss it as a trifle—a "tempest in a teapot," as one of our more conservative pundits succeeded in labeling it. Be that as you will, the "happening" I speak of came to be touted in its heyday as the Hadleyburg Renaissance, a denomination of uncertain origin, as far as I'm aware, but popularized by the university professor who appeared on one of the better known weeknight talk shows, and who explained to a public long ignorant of such matters—it was our own best known man of letters, he inserted, who once pointed out that those who did not read good books enjoyed no advantage over those who could not—that the authors who had instigated this most unlikely revival had taken as their models, or at least taken their inspiration from, certain landmarks in our literature, now largely forgotten.

At the outset of this affair it seems that Hadleyburg, a small city in the heartland some hundred miles from the metropolis in which I record these observations, had passed, by a strong majority, a piece of local ordinance which banned the use of tobacco in its restaurants. Scarcely a week had expired when there appeared in the town's morning news a letter to the editor, signed by one "H.M.," who, while declaring himself a non-smoker, "reformed and rehabilitated," decried the selfishness of a code which denied the smokers one night of the week—"nay, nor for a token generosity, a single evening of the month"—to avail themselves of the restaurants otherwise open to the public. He denounced the concern about secondhand smoke, given "the massive demolition of our earth and air," for an "unconscionable absurdity"; he admonished those who sincerely cared about the public health to "omit one bridge over the river, go round a little there, and throw up one arch at least over the darker gulf of ignorance and inequality which surrounds us"; and, lastly, he ranted about the pitfall of hypocrisy, imploring Heaven to "have mercy on us all—non-smokers and pagans alike—for we are all somehow dreadfully cracked about the head, and sadly need mending."

It took our talk show professor to inform the viewing public that this letter was replete with allusions, and that its writer had borrowed word for word, except for certain slight but significant alterations, from passages in the originals, which were to be found in books that he suggested everyone should know about—though he left it at that, with no further lessons on the originals themselves.[2] But unless as was later suspected by some, that the Hadleyburg Renaissance was the work of a single militant iconoclast, there must have been those who were seized by the spirit, if not by the scholarly references, of this seminal voice of dissent, for it served as the rallying cry for the revolt—or rather, the "tempest in the teapot"—which followed.

For the movement was soon publishing its own monthly journal, the memorable *Hadleyburg Literary Messenger*, which proved the catalyst for a variety of literary forms and entities. These were admittedly of uneven merit, and yet I suspect that the best of them survive, if only in obscure recesses there, within the consciousness of our age, notwithstanding the opinion to be encountered that ours is an age in which consciousness of these matters is peculiarly barren. There was, first of all, I remember, a certain "Modest Proposal" which suggested an outlandish but strangely appealing settlement for the war over smoking, and which was succeeded by two similarly perceptive polemics bearing the same title but straying from the confrontation at hand to engage larger, perhaps worthier issues—and thus portending the direction of the movement, as it developed. The second of these undertook to demonstrate how the pro-gun people among us might best employ their guns for the general good, while the third addressed the phenomenon of children begetting children, which was not the least confounding of our implacable vexations, and offered a practical solution to the problem which was strangely tempting—yet so barbarous in nature that I dare not be the one to detail its dark and troubling purport.

More sublimely, there next appeared a fine philosophical tract on the virtues of tolerance, much in the manner of Milton and Mill, according to our informative professor. Also, a long narrative poem, *The Oddities*, was launched in serialized installments, the poet allotting us a new "oddity" with each issue and exhibiting a decided bent for satire, for it bit rather too harshly to be patterned expressly after those noble epics of the ancients, yet it had soon gathered its considerable following. And although satire was at first the predominant mode to be encountered in the upstart *Messenger*, this gave way gradually to a groping lyricism, observable not only in the influx of lyric poetry but also in a revival of the informal, truly personal essay, all of which found, surprisingly, much to celebrate in our world as it was, and all of which did so, if inevitably with varying finesse, yet with genuine feeling.

Which brings me to what must be considered the finest accomplishment of this entire production, an achievement no less remarkable for its modest beginning, a rather conventional-looking sonnet which bore the rather unprepossessing title of "Gretel's Mother," or for the distracting burden of notoriety soon to be incurred with the revelation of its authorship, though this was tipped from the beginning in a cryptic way by the author's abbreviated signature, that by now intriguing "H.M."

On the surface, "Gretel's Mother" introduced the sad if somewhat tiresome theme of child abuse and abandonment, so that it was the wonderful music of the thing which first commanded attention—held us spellbound, to confess the truth. Cast in the form of a Shakespearean sonnet, it soon evolved into a series of these—they were shortly appearing two to the issue so that we had, in all, some twenty-one of them, not quite three hundred lines altogether, and yet by our paltry standards quite enough. In the end, then, we were given a sonnet sequence, complete with a "Who can she be?" motif, snaring us all the while in the Orphean enchantment of its song, compelling us to see and to feel anew, to partake of some larger and all pervading sense of human abandonment, as nearly as I can express it, of human hardship and woe. And love. Yes, the sonnets revealed to us much about the nature of love—oh, passion, yes, there was that to be sure within these verses, but that of a love which transcended. And they taught us to love the things of this life as well, for they sprang after all from the soil already cultivated by those lyric poems which had celebrated the world as it was, and, perhaps most telling, they cut against the grain of our wearisome and massive depressions, both economic and spiritual. And it may be worth adding that they contradicted, too, the jingoistic sentiment of the times, for as a matter of record it was maintained, in one corner at least, that the collective designation which the sequence had forthwith assumed, *The Serendipity Sonnets*, constituted a sly and seditious homage to the three princes of ancient Serendip, and thus to the very people who, confirmed in enmity against us and sensing the vulnerability we incurred with our endless domestic crises, added their insults to our injuries, so to speak, and baited us relentlessly.

But for my part, again, I found it unnecessary to dwell upon an interpretation as strained as that, with its subversive implications. Preferring to think simply that these *Serendipity Sonnets* were a wonderful and unforeseen gift, I could see how the gift, in its unobtrusive way, was healing us, enlightening us, till we perceived the grandeur of its humble charity. Perhaps we began to apprehend what the philosophers intended with their grandiose phrase, "the human condition," for the sonnets taught us—lifted us to—a knowledge of our humanity. To read them was to live again.

When they were completed we basked for awhile in their serene afterglow, scarcely aware that there was nothing of comparable genius to follow, scarcely noticing, until it was decidedly moribund, the movement's rapid decline. There is, in my judgment, but a single contribution during this final phase which remains worthy of mention here. "The Westward Inn," as it was called, portrayed in considerable detail an improbable haven for the hapless elderly, though I, for one, could never read to the conclusion of this apocalyptic fiction without transforming this title to "The Westward End" in my retention of it, and it may well be I should have read in this the foreshadowing clue to the movement's failing, or some consciousness from within it that the end was near.

And then, as suddenly and as inexplicably as it had begun, it seemed, the Hadleyburg Renaissance was over, leaving in its wake the effect, the impression of a dream. Inexplicably, yes, for with the exception of those who took the whole affair for a conspiracy—a sinister but failed tactic to "soften our will" and divert us from our "tried and true way of life," as they were fond of expressing it—no one has so far troubled to put forth an adequate explanation for its demise. Suffice it to say that one day we found ourselves gazing on its many accomplishments as on so many glowing embers scattered in darkness, its spark no longer combustible with those rarefied elements, whatever they might have been, which for the course of almost but not quite two years had fired its imaginative energy.

And here I would be remiss if I did not elaborate upon that final theory of authorship which I have seen fit to mention, for there were those, again, who took this revelation when it occurred as confirmation for their suspicions that the whole of this literary performance, despite its stunning variety and richness, was the work of a single conspirator. I myself counted it at first as nothing better than a rumor born of that darkness settling upon us once again. The purest conjecture, I wanted to label it, but there it was: the revelation, carried in the Sunday Supplement of our leading news organ,[3] in a weekly column by a woman who researches just such riddles, that the once mysterious H.M. was probably never intended to be the allusion divined by a few of us, but in reality a reference to none other than the infamous Hans Maladeux. To which, if anyone had cried incredible, I would have hastened to concur. I will not, I cannot explain how I came around at last to brood upon this strange hypothesis. For it was more than a hypothesis according to the reporter who propounded it, and whose investigation, notwithstanding the fact that her subject had been orphaned early in life, seemed thoroughgoing and convincing, and revealed for us that the proper given name of this slippery personage was likely Hansford, although there was compelling evidence, as well, to suggest that the more common appellation in this instance was actually a shortened form of Hansel.

Further, it was discovered that the surname was his own invention, in all probability a corruption of some more common and less flamboyant lineage, but making it virtually impossible to ascertain the existence of a sister, let alone a sister named Gretel.

But no matter the lineage. It was this sudden unmasking of the man himself that so amazed us. Could this embittered malcontent, this lunatic fanatic, this—yes, let's out with it—this proven criminal, now have proven himself a man of humane letters? A master of deceit, rather, as some persist? He could indeed, you say, have penned that inflammatory letter to the editor in Hadleyburg, and yes, I'll grant that's plausible, but was this same incendiary then the poet behind those edifying sonnets inscribed with similar initials, that masterpiece which marked the apex of our days and moved, they say, even our beleaguered President to cry "Eureka!" when it first appeared? Does not the assumption call for the prematurely balding Maladeux to be now styled in comely Elizabethan locks and curls? Or more to the point, does it not presuppose a paroled or fugitive Maladeux, a Maladeux reformed and somehow rehabilitated, a Maladeux (hallelujah) reborn? And yet, come to think, is not just such a supposition within the ken of anyone who has read—nay, lived—*The Serendipity Sonnets*? Of anyone, that is, who, forsaking common sense, has made the leap that gets beyond our preconceptions, and glimpsed the knowledge that Maladeux, and all his kind, are in the end no different from the rest of us?

These are questions which, as your recorder, merely, I leave unanswered. Posterity, in its time, may grapple with them—or not, as it sees fit. Much will depend, I predict, upon the survival of the spirit of our "teapot" Renaissance, for in the flesh I do pronounce it dead.

And now, be it known, life reverts to a meanness heretofore unpublicized, or so it seems to me. I cannot speak for others, but once again I wake to find the noise of rude disturbance in the streets. Publicly there's no discussion of it yet, but there it is, a constant threat, a constant factor in our lives.

Quite early one morning on my walk I had a look at a group of the offenders. They were but one group among many such, no doubt, but there they were in person—not that disembodied and malicious merriment that floats over rooftops and drifts up the avenues with the first intimations of dawn, waiting to prove itself the desecration of a splendid summer day. Beneath some trees in the corner of the otherwise deserted parking lot of the high school, they were loading their sleeping bags and who can say what other paraphernalia into their dilapidated microbus. They detected my presence a good block away, and there followed a burst of yelling and hilarity which I tried successfully not to understand. I walked on by, and soon they were passing me in turn with their radio blaring its wild mumbo jumbo, malign and unintelligible.

They would not be going far, I suspected, given the nearly prohibitive cost of fuel, but I could well surmise their intention to join the droves who now sought exodus from cities such as ours. For somewhere a nerve had been touched: a rumor, dubious at first, but irrevocable and ever widening, warned how our enemies, now multiplied and stronger, conspired to turn the tables, so to speak, and bomb us at their will. And so began this massive shuffle to evacuate our bulging population centers—a movement quite the opposite, it's true, of that which transpired in the harrowing times I endeavored to portray near the beginning of this narrative.[4]

As for me, I keep recalling the words of one of our leaders, delivered at the height of our short-lived Renaissance. "Nothing," he exclaimed, "has ever lifted our standard of living as much as this mutual goodwill of those who are doing the living." He spoke, they say, with light in his eyes, and there were those who foresaw in the moment the dawning of a new era. Yet nowadays, alas, the honest recorder is bound to acknowledge that the reverse of his proposition is also true.

For nowadays, sadly, it's seldom if ever that one encounters even a friendly dog, such as I remember from those days when the *Sonnets* were in vogue... But enough, and, once again, I cannot proceed further, for I won't malign a species to whom I, for one, am greatly beholden. Can it be, as has been elsewhere claimed, they comprehend us better than the philosophers? Yes, I can believe that the best of them do, yet in ways of their own—about which we seem to know little.

---

1. I draw no conclusions from the fact, and simply note here that this was a flight quite the reverse of those who in older times fled from pestilence, and in the present instance a flight perhaps as improvident as it was shameful, for while intensifying the already sadly depressed aspect of the dwindling provinces, it served only to exacerbate the nearly intolerable burdens of the already teeming cities.

2. It may be worth noting, however, that a number of us, perhaps more practiced than the average reader, found cause to infer a further allusion from the choice of initials which the writer of the letter in question elected to inscribe it with.

3. It should be remarked here that the story was seized upon and carried as well by those countless popular tabloids which deal exclusively with the sensational, a phenomenon which in our time may well parallel the surfeit of superstition and unfounded prognostication which marked older but similarly dark periods of human history.

4. I must here insert that I, too, took part in this second migration (just as I had in that other, as you may have deducted). I count myself no hero, yet I had, after all, the survival of my report to consider. Then too, I often found myself longing for those headier days of my youth, when I went westering as summer called. I made my reservation, hoarded some fuel, and as the days preceding our zero hour dwindled and others scattered in all directions, I drove west in a Rent-A-Wreck.

Dilsey's Story: "Is This How It Is Now?"

Whenever I was feeling lost and low, I learned somewhere late in the middle of my life to look to the birds of the field, or better yet, when I happened to come across it, to heed the counsel of our own native poet, Walt Whitman, when he wrote "I loaf and invite my soul." Such counsel I may have taken to heart, unconsciously, when I formed the habit of rising early in the small mountain city of Flagstaff, in northern Arizona, and walking the mile downtown to the Station House for my morning coffee and back, refusing all the while to give a concentrated thought to anything and instead allowing my mind to loaf for at least this hour and entertain me as it would. I have been grateful for this habit which persisted with the years, enabling me to glimpse from time to time the gift of life apart from the demands of mere survival.

On one such morning in early spring, near the beginning of my seventy-third year, I puffed my way up the hill on Beaver Street toward my now empty home—my wife had passed away the year before and my two surviving sons were now well settled in Seattle, where they had worked their way through graduate school. I don't recall my reverie on that particular morning, only that I was experiencing a growing need to look behind me, a premonition that I was being dogged by someone or something. Discarding the wisdom of a famous ball player, I paused to catch my breath, and turned my head slowly to survey the street below me. Nothing, at first, but then, about to resume my climb, I discovered that behind a clump of newly sprung daffodils in a yard just two houses back there was indeed a dog, apparently keeping an eye on me. A beagle, or some sort of mix, it may have been, for although her coloring was right and her ears were hanging down, her legs seemed a little too long. "Her," I've said, because yes, I was also able to discern her gender as she relieved herself beyond the flower bed, still watching me all the while.

A gift of fate, I suddenly realized—a gift I had done nothing to earn, mind you—was presenting itself to me, following me home from the Station House, it may have been, that coffee house downtown where almost two years before I had ditched the dog who followed me in the opposite direction. He'd been distracted by some pigeons just as I dodged into the shop, and as I sat behind the window sipping my coffee I had to watch him looking for me again, but without success.

Out of a sense of guilt I searched for him later at the shelter on the edge of town, and though I never found him, what I found instead was a calling that began that same day, as a volunteer to walk the lost, the strayed, and the abandoned impounded in that same shelter. My year-long tenure ended badly, however, the fault of my own hesitation to adopt a dog who, unknown to me, was about to be euthanized. And so I left off on my good karma, it may have been, an adventure which was healing a nagging depression, a sharpened awareness of aging and loneliness which had beset me with the passing of my wife.

Now, I saw, I was being offered this second chance, coming from the opposite direction, a reprieve I hardly deserved, but which I at once sought not to squander. She detoured often to sniff the grass and foliage, whatever was handy, and yet she was careful to pull up close behind me, as if to pass herself off as a long lost friend—a canine tactic with which I was by then familiar. When I stopped of a sudden, bent to stroke her and speak to her softly—trying this time, I admit, to put my best foot forward—she seemed to welcome my attentions and even licked me lightly on the hand.

Thus was born a lifetime of close companionship between us. "Lifetime," I say, which indeed it was for her, though for me, to be more accurate, it was sixteen and one-half years. Thus she was young and I was old as our paths first crossed, and I had at that time, early on, to decide upon a name for her. Because her feet were small and rabbit-like the name of "Lucky" crossed my mind, yet this was just too common and frivolous, I considered at once, for this uncommon dog. I had to think again, and I recalled from my time with the shelter one or two dogs whom she resembled just a little, and who were referred to as Southern hounds. And thus it was that I decided at last to consult a southern novel, and there in the first I turned to, Faulkner's *The Sound and the Fury*, I came across a character named "Dilsey." I had never known anyone named Dilsey, yet it seemed simple and easy, neither too common nor pretentious, and so came about the name we abided by for the rest of her years.

I was wrong, however, to think the name "simple and easy," for those who inquired were invariably baffled by it. "What, Guilty?" or "What, Dulce?" they would attempt, almost annoyed, until finally along came a stranger who, in his own way, reassured me once and for all.

He was a pleasant, well dressed young man with dark curly hair who paused outside the Station House to exchange a few words with me and Dilsey, settled at our outside table. We spoke of the welcome warmth for early February, our first Chinook, it may have been, promising spring. Having expressed his liking for my dog, he then moved to the question I was anticipating.

"Dilsey," I offered. To my great relief, he smiled knowingly, repeating the name deliberately and lovingly, it seemed.

"Oh, are you from Virginia?" he wanted to know.

"I spent my first five years in West Virginia," I allowed, "but I'm in debt to William Faulkner, of Mississippi—a place I've never been, I confess—for the name. I consider myself a Southwesterner at heart," I added, "where I've lived most of my life."

He smiled knowingly again, with perhaps a touch of nostalgia for his own Virginia. He spoke again to Dilsey softly by her name, then stepped inside for his morning coffee.

I took it he was on his way to an office job somewhere in the downtown area in which we lingered, but I never saw him again. Yet I never worried again, either, about the name I had bestowed on my dog, which seemed always right thereafter.

I might here add that Dilsey's habit to investigate, to sniff the environment tirelessly and then stand with her head raised as if thinking it over, led me to assign a facetious last name, "Sniffinger," but I confined this surname to formal occasions only, of which there were few.

One such occasion, however, developed when I took her for her first checkup and used her full name to introduce her to our new vet—whose own name I've forgotten, although I well recall his words. He deduced that she was somewhere in her second year, "but not a day over two," he declared. "And already spayed," he observed. "I'd say at about six months. Well muscled, too, at an even thirty pounds—decidedly middle-sized. You sure can pick 'em."

"But it was she who salvaged me," I intervened. "A gift of fate, I think of it. And she arrived house-broken, too. Even if without a collar."

As we speculated on her breed he agreed that she was at least half beagle. Tri-colored, tan and black on white, she had the right coloring down to the white tip on her tail, which she never lost, although her tail was always a bit bushier than that of the usual beagle. She had also a beagle's floppy ears, but only about half the normal length, and coming to a point instead of rounding off. Yet in her youth her eyes, brown and inquisitive, seemed almond-shaped and beagle-like whenever she looked at me, as she often did in those early days, as if to comprehend or sometimes question me.

But there was something else in her as well. Her legs were too long for those of a beagle, for one thing. She loved to go bounding like a deer when she was off the leash and the occasion permitted. If we came to a grassy field that was vacant—or even a vacant parking lot on a Sunday would do—I'd let her go bounding, and then I'd crouch down like an ogre and advance on her just to watch her start circling hard around me. As I pivoted to face her the circles got faster and closer, until finally she dared to brush past me with such swiftness that I did well to tag her as she went by. Off leash, she always looked at me when I called, then waited patiently for me to come to her and attach it again. I came to see, and sometimes had to explain to others, that she had always had "her own agenda," as it were. I did not mind this trait in her, and I came to prefer it just as she did. There was no "master" in our relationship.

Once on a weekend we went to a nearby schoolyard that was deserted except for a youth just leaving with a football tucked under his arm. I had just unleashed her when he approached and asked to pet her. He did, and then watched in breathless wonder while she performed her circling feat, wild and passionate, until she finally tired and halted at a little distance to see what we thought.

"Wow," the boy stammered. "Where do you get a dog like that?"

1 had to consider, but then tried to explain.

"You just have to be lucky. Sometimes it's just a matter of fate, you know."

When she was six we sold our home and moved from the Southwest, where I had lived for six decades, to the Northwest, where my sons, Loren and Tim, were residing, along with my daughters-in-law, and my granddaughter, Della Rayne—Tim's daughter. It was a relocation they had urged since I had become a widower, and as I aged I had begun to see the wisdom of it, though I wondered how Dilsey would take it. I was ready to "downsize," as the saying went, and simplify, if possible. I was retired, after all, and I sold our home for perhaps less than 1 should have. A year later, after arriving, I also sold our car, aware of my incompetence in the vast and often congested traffic of the big city, but also to counter the steep cost of living and consequent hardship which Seattle exacted on its middle class—not to mention its poor who survived under its bridges and in substandard housing, including tents strewn among the trees around certain freeway interchanges.

Yet I cannot say that we ever regretted the move. This was a land of mountains and forests and waterways to which my remaining family introduced us. It was here that Dilsey experienced what must have been her first encounter with an ocean. On an Oregon beach she sniffed to her heart's content, and at the water's edge stared seaward, thinking it over, one could tell. Here, too, she bounded like her old self after the yellow tennis ball we tossed for her along the packed wet sand where the waves came in, though she was careful to dodge those waves all the while. At the end of our excursion we snapped a photo of her, a portrait of a fatigued yet nonetheless exhilarated canine, with footprints of both man and dog in the sand beside her, with her ears laid slightly back, her mouth slightly open, and her eyes rolled slightly left and upward. I'll call here upon a poet whom I read long ago, and borrow the better part of a line of his which Dilsey brought to mind:

...the seal's wide spindrift gaze toward paradise.[1]

And surely, for all the world, her gaze seemed to be inquiring, "Is this how it is now? Is this how it's going to be?"

Could I have answered yes, then heaven, it may have been, was all around us even then.

By the time Dilsey was twelve she passed me up for the first time, in terms of dog years, that is. Without our car I'd have errands I had to run alone sometimes, so that I'd begin to worry if gone too long, but upon my return I'd most often find her rising from her nap to look at me with love in her eyes. There were just a few times, however, when I opened the door in time to catch her making rapidly toward her bed. I had to deduce that she had been waiting for me just inside the door, but also that she preferred I didn't know this. Just another aspect of her independence, I had to infer. It was an attitude she bore until the end.

Without the car, we had taken to walking even more. From the time we landed on Southwest Morgan Street in West Seattle, we would trek down and then back up the steep incline which that street provided, this time to the nearest Starbuck's instead of the Station House, but nonetheless for another round trip of two miles. It was always good to have a destination such as that, and we would sit together at an outside table year around, bundled up in the winter—Dilsey in a coat of rough blue flannel with a velcro hitch and I in my big blue parka. People, and sometimes people with their dogs, would begin to see us as regulars, and Dilsey made us a number of friends—because yes, it was Dilsey, I noticed, that they were first attracted to. Her face had turned from mostly tan to mostly white by then, and the almond shape of her eyes had disappeared, and yet she was still a beauty, I'm inclined to add.

Often the question would arise, "How old is she?"

"1 think about thirteen," I'd reply at the time I speak of, offering my opinion based on that of our vet back in Flagstaff. Whenever this brought surprise, I liked to proceed with my usual response.

"It's just a question of time," I'd say, "as to who's going to outlast who," explaining how she had just in the last year passed by me in her dog years.

Politely, they might feign surprise again.

"It must be all the walking," they would offer.

As for the whiteness of Dilsey's face, I had hardly noticed the gradual change. It was for our new vet, Dr. Wen, to point it out, in her thoughtful way. On our first visit we briefly discussed her possible parentage, and a week later she sent me a newspaper clipping containing a photograph of a mature red heeler, an Australian cattle dog who, given up for lost, had made the news with one of those miraculous journeys to return home again. The red heeler, she added in her note, was bred from the blue heeler and the wild dingo, and she left it at that. But I saw her intention, for immediately I recognized the likeness of Dilsey, as she had aged, to the dog pictured in the article. It took me by surprise, but there was the whitening face, the longer legs, even the ears, for Dilsey's were always pointed, and on occasion now stood straight up when she was lying or sleeping on her side. Moreover, the wild dingo in her background could provide me with some explanations I was glad to ponder—her instinct for independence, or "her own agenda," as I liked to express it, and a certain reluctance to appear too demonstrative. These were revelations by which I came to understand and appreciate.

And as for "all the walking" we were doing, we were in truth walking an average of twice the two miles we traveled round trip for morning coffee. There was a park just next door to our apartment building, but because it was usually busy and often noisy, it offered little of leisurely solitude, so that we preferred other destinations. We could, for instance, turn south on 35th Avenue after a single block on Morgan, and then, after a block of shops and offices—one of which housed Dr. Wen—we could take our time up another hill, not as steep as the one home from Starbuck's, and after a mile, arrive at a tiny coffee house called Cafe Osita (Little Bear). We could detect this quaint oasis from a long two blocks away when our tree-lined sidewalk leveled out and the big red umbrella above its single outside table became visible. There, seated comfortably with my dog and my coffee, we were made welcome by the young proprietors, Michael and Andrea, who never failed to provide Dilsey with a treat or two, and, even when busy, extend the warmth of their smiles and friendly conversation. It was yet another instance where Dilsey earned us two good friends.

This was an attribute which 1 myself had always seemed to lack. It may have been I tried too hard when young, and then, enjoying little success, I failed to try much at all. I thus had much to learn from Dilsey, who seemed so able to befriend without really trying, but just by being herself. I suspected there was much in which we complemented one another, and that she sensed this as well as I did. Could it be, as has been suggested well over a century ago by our greatest man of letters, that our dogs comprehend us "better than the philosophers"? And yes, I tend to believe that the best of them do, if only in ways of their own—about which we seem to know little.

In addition to the two-mile loop to Cafe Osita, there was another, shorter alternative of about a mile that we liked to take, especially on rare sunny days. We could head in the opposite direction and after a couple of blocks connect with a path which led to and circled a wide duck pond and offered a view of the Seattle skyline and the Cascades beyond. The pond was fed by a natural source called Longfellow Creek, which emerged from a hillside and rushed among landscaped boulders and flora beside steps with a sturdy railing, and I recall some fine spring days when, having completed this short descent, we rested on a sunny bench, watching the returning swallows circling above and skimming the pond while the unconcerned ducks paddled around with their young in tow. As spring turned to summer and the swallows moved on, there were always the airliners overhead. Out of earshot so as not to disturb us unless we cared to watch them, they slowly descended at carefully planned intervals like great silver birds reflecting the light in the sky, seeking the earth again—but back beyond our range of vision, at SeaTac Terminal.

In such golden hours I counted life good for both of us, and the years slipped by as we kept, by and large, to these three favored walks. And yet one morning before we began, feeling stiff and a little sore, I heard a complaint escape my lips before I thought about it.

"Oh Dilsey," I sighed. "We're both getting old."

She looked at me without surprise.

Inevitably, of course, changes were beginning to show. I was made ever more wary of a tender and swollen right knee, the result of an old injury, I suspected, and, more telling, my voice was beginning to fade, so that I had often to clear my throat or even cough in trying to right it.

Worse yet, near the middle of her fifteenth year, Dilsey suffered what I took to be a stroke. Returning from a walk on a late summer day she seemed to be losing her balance, listing to her left, even falling on her side, and looking at me with both wonder and desperation in her eyes. I gathered her into my arms and rushed her to Dr. Wen, our nearby vet. Diagnosing at once, she administered an anti-inflamatory injection, which, coupled with a relaxant, brought immediate relief. She suspected that a tumor on the left side of Dilsey's brain had acted up in the heat and her exertion. She must have been right, because the problem never recurred.

Dilsey, 1 am certain, understood the emergency and offered no objection to our unplanned visit, nor even to being carried on this occasion. I, for my part, tapered off on the length of our walks thereafter.

She lived for three more years. Although it was a position she had almost never assumed before, she now chose to sit whenever she could. The tail she used to hoist straight up behind her, white tip at the top, was now sadly drooping, though the white tip remained. Her hearing seemed to decline, which could have been the effect, in part, of my own flagging voice, but even when I was able to whistle she invariably looked in the wrong direction. Her eyesight, too, caused me concern, reminding me of the cataract surgery I myself had required. She tended to bump into obstructions in our apartment, which was admittedly small for the two of us, but objects which had offered no previous trouble kept getting in her way, and she sought out corners and the shelter under tables she had not sought before. Then too, whenever I bent over the kitchen sink or counter while preparing my meals, I'd feel her wedging herself between me and the counter, not to get by, apparently, but as if to remind me of her presence. I'd reach to scratch her head or behind her ears, which she might tolerate briefly, but only to retreat, shake herself thoroughly, and amble away.

The gesture called to mind a curious habit she maintained for as long as I knew her. Whenever we found ourselves in a group of several persons, as at the home of one son or the other, I'd feel her nose bump suddenly against my leg, but only to see her retreating before I could acknowledge her presence—or rather, assure her of my own presence in the crowd, for that, I came to understand, was what she was checking on, trusting her nose with that quick but unmistakable bump.

On one such occasion I was obliged to take a ferry across the Sound to Port Townsend and back, an appointment which would necessitate my absence for the better part of the day. Loren and Lee, my daughter-in-law, kindly drove us to the ferry dock that Saturday morning, then took Dilsey with them to their home, with its large fenced back yard, for the rest of the day. There, later on, I should add, Tim and Debbie, and also Della Rayne and her friend, were to join us for dinner that evening. By the time I returned, making use of a cab from the ferry dock, the guests had all arrived and Lee, coming forward, was quick to tell me that Dilsey had been looking all day for me, going from room to room and into the yard and back. Yet when she summoned her Dilsey merely stood looking, and I had to wonder whether there wasn't a bit of resentment in her holding back. But I recognized that warmth in her eyes, and as I advanced she decided to meet me half way. She greeted me with that terse but decided bump of the nose on my leg, then turned away, trying to seem casual, I could see. But that bump of the nose I was by then familiar with, and though it was her means of making sure it was me, I came in time to think it was also, in her own reserved and undemonstrative way, a gesture of affection, as if to say "I'm glad you're here," and perhaps even more.

Dilsey always slept well at night, and now she gradually took to sleeping more of the day. Her bed was a shallow wicker basket which I had found at a thrift shop. I had an old pillow which served as the perfect mattress. I covered it with a couple of fluffy but frayed old towels which I could launder easily, and for winters I had an old flannel blanket in which she like to snuggle, often with an audible sigh, or even adding a slight licking of her lips if I could cover her gently without disturbing her.

I could never break my own habit of rising early, at first light, and often now when I hoped to rouse her, I could see that she was not up to making it that morning. I tried once or twice to place my hand beneath her belly, so warm and soft, and gently lift, but her eyes hardly opened and her body remained limp. I hadn't the heart to force her, and so she took to "sleeping in," as I explained to those who noticed her absence on my walks to Starbuck's, now taken alone. There was always the Sound down below and the lights on Southworth Harbor across it, the Olympic Mountains just beginning to show behind them, and sometimes the moon might be up above me, westering through the clouds and lighting the waters of the Sound. It was all too beautiful to miss, and yet it was never the same without Dilsey.

On one such morning, as I labored back up the hill after coffee just as the winter sun was about to clear the horizon, a car which I recognized pulled over to the curb beside me. The driver was a man of color and gentle manner who had stopped twice before.

"Sir," he addressed me, leaning over with his window down, "Sir, is your dog all right? I've seen you before with her, you remember. Is she doing all right?"

I assured him that she was.

"Just sleeping in a lot these days. Getting old, you know," I tried to explain.

"Oh, that's good." He seemed relieved, smiling now. "I'm glad to know she's still with you," he concluded, and he rejoined the flow of traffic.

There are good souls to be discovered in this life, I couldn't help thinking, perhaps all around us, and more than we realize.

Although she was missing the early morning walks, Dilsey was still good for the second, as long as we took our time. Having cut back on the length of our excursions, we seldom made it to Café Osita, but would more often stop short of that former destination to turn east for a block to a much less traveled 34th Avenue, a side street lined by neatly kept homes on lots with fifty-foot frontages, all of which were dressed with lawns and flower beds behind the retaining wall along our sidewalk. Sometimes we would halt altogether and just observe—or sniff and observe, in Dilsey's case—as when we reached the bottom of the hill on 34th, already close to home, and stood before a large vacant field on our right. "Vacant," I say, and yet there were three stately oaks, each in its own corner and each enjoyed by crows and squirrels, and Dilsey had tall stems of grass and wildflowers to sniff and contemplate. She did her best, and I could see she was smiling, as dogs will sometimes smile. In spite of a life spent mostly on a leash she never seemed to lose her sense of wonder. It was I, on the other end of the leash, who for much of my life had neglected to loaf and invite my soul, as the poet counseled, and who, once again, had much to learn from my dog.

She was the same around the duck pond, where grass and flora were thriving and swallows were skimming the water again. We would seek our bench in the sunshine, where she would lie down at my feet, then ease into my shadow and pant lightly with her eyes partly closed. Yes, we would soon be retreating, but I could see she was smiling again. Such moments warmed my heart, and I resolved to stick to our routine as long as we could—for as long, that is, as she retained the capacity to enjoy what was left of her life.

Dilsey's last year may have been marred by pain I was slow in perceiving, for there were those who took issue with my judgment—friends, I thought, who told me I should be able to see that my dog was suffering, and it was time to end it. There was even a man in his car who honked his horn when we were slow to cross the street, and the woman beside him who yelled as they passed, "Put that dog away, you idiot!"

I was relieved, under the circumstances, when I found in my mailbox a reminder from our vet that it was time for her rabies booster—a summons which would afford me a chance for a consultation.

"Well," Dr. Wen announced, following a cursory examination, "her heart's still good, but I don't see the need for the boosters any longer," she added, her voice turning solemn. "She was limping a little when you came in, Charlie, and her hind legs are stiffened and probably arthritic. She's seventeen now, if I remember rightly, and probably suffering some pain."

She left her desk to search a cabinet and produced a bottle of pills for me.

"You might try these. They sometimes help."

I hadn't the presence of mind to say that she wouldn't swallow pills and couldn't be tricked, but as if remembering, she continued.

"I wouldn't make an issue of it," she advised. "Just break a tablet in half and drop it in her feed once a day."

I nodded, but moved to the topic most on my mind.

"But doctor," I asked, "how will I know when...and can I bring her here if her time comes?"

She smiled, but only slightly, it being a question doubtless familiar to her, but nevertheless not easily dealt with.

"She'll probably let you know about that."

"But she never moans or whimpers, not even in her sleep, as far as I know."

"Some dogs don't," she allowed. "Just make her comfortable when you can." Hesitating, she produced a small card from a drawer in her desk, where she had seated herself again.

"And yes," she added, "you can bring her in when it's time. But there's also an alternative." She handed me the calling card she had located.

"4 for Paws," I read. I recalled that Tim and Debbie, having endured the necessity of putting down their own dog, Tucker, had turned to this same alternative.

"They're four colleagues," she explained. "All licensed vets. They come to your place," she added. "Some feel it's more humane, more compassionate that way."

1 tried to study the card, but without much success.

"Yes, I can see how it would be," I finally thought to say.

Weeks passed as we approached the end of summer. I had our twenty-by-twenty-inch floor fan going much of the time, which Dilsey seemed to appreciate. She slept long and peacefully, ate a little now and then—and, oddly enough, swallowed the medicinal tablets mixed in her food without issue, just as the doctor had foreseen.

Our walks were short, usually just over to the park next door, sometimes merely around the parking lot. Yet one fine morning the day dawned bright and Dilsey was on her feet as soon as I was. It crossed my mind that there was something magical at work.

Outside, she hesitated, lifted her head and sniffed around awhile. Having decided, she gave me a look, then fell in behind me and followed with steady resignation. We were headed down to Starbuck's for one last time, and together again.

It was a Sunday, the morning remaining bright and beautiful, and the traffic was light. I had to help her over a curb or two, but all along the way 1 quietly rejoiced in her company. I admit to rehearsing to myself a "Look who's with me this morning" greeting for those whom we knew and might encounter. But arriving at Starbuck's, Dilsey got behind the chair I had chosen and stood facing the wall below the window, as though she would as soon go unnoticed in her condition. I should have understood, I reflected, and I had almost finished my coffee when it looked as though she might have her wish. It was early Sunday, after all, and like the traffic in the streets, pedestrians on the walks were few.

We were about to depart when I spotted down the walk an elderly lady, whose name escaped me just then, in the company of her German shepherd, Ben. He was old and somewhat undersized for his breed, and his demeanor suggested he had somewhere endured a life which was not without hardship. He always stepped carefully with his head lowered, as though preferring to pass unnoticed—not unlike Dilsey on that particular morning.

"Well, hello there, Charlie" sang Mary Ellen—her name coming back to me suddenly. "So nice to see you two together again!"

"One more time, we decided," but just then she saved me from anything more.

"Well, will you look at that!" she exclaimed.

I looked, and saw, remarkably, that Ben had not only stopped to stare, as if recognizing a long lost friend, but was now wagging his tail. And no less wondrous, there was Dilsey, turned from the wall to face him, now lifting her tail from its droop to offer a token wag in return, as though in appreciation of this unexpected affection—and from one not unlike herself in ways both may have understood.

We stared at one another, all four of us, speechless in that magic moment.

Back home, and thoroughly spent, Dilsey slept soundly the rest of the morning, while I had time to reflect. Could it be, after all, that life was never meant to be prolonged? Could it be love, be it only in a passing glance or a wag of the tail, that was meant to prevail? Could it be, despite the pain, that Dilsey—and Ben—had taught me something again? I couldn't help but recall the bumper stickers I'd been seeing on just a few cars: "Wag, don't bark."

Dilsey lost all appetite after that day, a development I had been wary of. Try as I might, I could encourage only a nibble now and then. I started to call "4 for Paws," changed my mind, but soon decided again to call, and set an appointment for the following week.

With Dilsey asleep, I decided to shop at a convenience store close by. Upon my return I found her still sleeping, but now with her legs splayed out, just a couple of feet from her water bowl. I pushed the bowl closer, lifted her gently while she drank a little, then helped her back to her bed.

I called "4 for Paws" again to ask to move the appointment closer. I was put on hold, but the kindly secretary soon was back: a Dr. Ellison could come tomorrow, she said.

"Expect her about eleven a.m. She'll call you first."

On her last day, toward the end of what was probably her eighteenth summer, the morning broke mostly clear, and thinking we had ample time I led her slowly to the park across the street, where we settled on a bench in the sunshine. The park seemed peaceful, it being morning and the middle of the week, and we sat quietly for awhile, with Dilsey relaxed at my feet.

"The sun feels good," I said to her as I had said many times before when we were situated just as we were that morning, but perhaps more slowly this time, and with a trifle more emphasis on my final syllable.

She rolled her head around at that, and with bleary eyes gave me a look which I took for agreement. Yet she held the long look a moment longer as if wanting to say something more, and I was made aware somehow of the photograph I still cherished from her first day at the beach, which seemed long ago. The eyes were bleary now, but still they touched upon that old question, "Is this how it is now?" The youthful joy, the "wide spindrift gaze" conveyed in that old portrait was missing now, yet well remembered, a part of both of us, and the answer to the question, which I am sure we both comprehended in that expanded moment, still held true: Yes, this was how it is now.

Slowly I led and coaxed her back toward home. My cell phone rang in the process—Dr. Ellison, informing me she would be arriving at the appointed hour. Dilsey settled in her bed when we returned, and I tried to make everything ready.

She was sleeping near the wall which held my bookcases, collapsed on her left side, when I heard the knock of Dr. Ellison, a tall and comely woman with blond hair, though I cannot say much about her age or countenance, my own eyes perhaps a little bleary by then.

She was gentle and efficient, setting down her kit and a blanket and presenting her card, headed "4 for Paws" again, but this time bearing her name only. We discussed several matters, deciding, among other things, that "the remains," Dilsey's ashes, were to be scattered in an old apple orchard which their group had purchased on the edge of Yakima, Washington, just east of the Cascades, where sunlight prevailed.

As she at last made ready the injections, she looked to me quietly, and only acted when I nodded. The first was intended only to relax her and induce a deep sleep. 1 watched as Dilsey eased open her eye—I could see only her right one—as though still asleep. I saw it gradually roll back in her head, her breathing still steady. Dr. Ellison looked to me again, and I nodded.

Deftly, she found the vein which she sought in Dilsey's hind leg, eased in the needle and secured it with gauze and white tape. We watched as the breathing gradually stopped. There was no pain that I could detect, nor any contraction.

Dr. Ellison placed Dilsey in the small velvet blanket she had brought and asked if I wanted to carry her. I told her I did.

We made our way down the hallway toward our exit, and as she held the door and I stepped out I felt Dilsey's head flop loosely from beneath her blanket. Quickly, I supported the neck gone limp with my upturned wrist, and as 1 held her head in my cupped hand I sensed, all at once, the pity of her death.

I staggered slowly across the driveway to our parking lot, my bad right knee threatening to buckle, and as Dr. Ellison opened the hatchback to the car we sought, I placed my dog carefully on the padded bedding there. I straightened up and blinked, and then, seizing my last chance, I bent over again and held my face firmly against Dilsey's, our last space in time together, too late, I knew, to say goodbye, but nevertheless....

Straightening myself again, I had nearly lost my balance when I felt the doctor's arms enfold and brace me. I tried to say "thank you" a couple of times, but, given my unreliable voice, I am not sure that I made myself audible. In truth, I seemed both blinded and choked. Yet I made my way back to the curbing across the driveway, where I turned to wave goodbye.

Dr. Ellison also paused in her car, with Dilsey in the back, to wave a long goodbye, then slowly merged with the traffic and soon disappeared.

I won't forget her kindness.

---

1. Hart Crane, from *Voyages II*

Readers Guide

"Youth"

1. What were the Cities of Cibola? What was Coronado seeking in 1541 when he led his expedition as far as the high plains of Kansas? What, by comparison, are the two main characters in "Youth" seeking?

2. What is the dominant mood at the beginning of this story? When and how does it shift? What do you make of the paragraph, third from the end, that begins "But as for heaven"? What details in the following paragraph signal a darkening mood? Why is the elderly woman sitting alone in the light of her kitchen window "raising a spoon to her lips" instead of a fork?

3. Why can we assume that "drifting" is part of the nature of the narrator?

"Family Album"

1. Who is the narrator of this story—or, in literary terms, what is the "narrative perspective" or "point of view"? Compare this point of view to the "I" narrative, or "first person" point of view employed in "Youth," a perspective which imposes limited omniscience upon the narrator—note that in the last paragraph the narrator admits "I could never be sure just what she thought of me." By comparison, what are the advantages of the omniscient, and shifting, point of view in this story? What are the disadvantages of each? What purpose are the roman numerals serving as they divide this story into its parts?

2. Why is the title "Family Album"? How many family members, other than the husband and wife of the first story, are introduced in this story? What are their names? How do we know the last name of the family? Can we assume that some years have passed between the two opening stories? How many, approximately? In the long part V of this story, can you identify two incidents which might be called "flashbacks" in the main character's consciousness?

3. In what sense is the attempted reunion of the parents with their oldest son,

Loren, successful at the end of this story? Because this final part VIII is told from the wife's perspective, what is gained in the depiction of the story's final scene?

"The Eighth World of Royden Taul"

1. How is this story linked to the previous one? The character who refers to himself as "I" throughout is Charles Graves, aka "Charlie," but is he the main character (i.e., the "protagonist"), or is it the character named in the title, Royden Taul? If the latter, should not we call this a first person point of view with "limited omniscience," which might explain the difficulty of Graves and the others in fathoming the character of Royden Taul?

2. What is the meaning of the idiom "Down in the Mouth"? How could this meaning relate to the narrator's digression in part VI and Royden's occasional lapse into a "natural frown," which seems "the single blemish in a countenance which otherwise bespoke the best goodwill" and which exposes "some deeper complication"? What topic always seems to revive and renew him?

3. The narrator seems alert to Royden's every word with interest and respect, while the youngest member of the company, Matt Heyman, seldom takes him seriously. "Jesus," he remarks, "for a minute there I thought it was going to be 'commit the crime of your choice'" (section VII), and later (section VIII) when it seems that Royden has disappeared while trying to cross a busy boulevard because he believes the roiling traffic will part and wait for him, Matt laughs it off with "missing person...Call the police." Is there unconscious irony in his frivolous use of "Jesus" and "missing person"?

"Llano Country"

1. By what reference in the previous story is this one introduced, and what, in turn, is this story soon introducing? Royden Taul refers to "the llano country of New Mexico, land of abandoned homesteads, desolate and wonderful;" can desolation be wonderful? What is the mood throughout?

2. Note that the narrator describes Perdido's buildings as "all lined up and ready, just as you'd expect to see them," and then again in the next paragraph as "all things you'd expect and want to see there." What building, however, seems to be the one exception? What is the meaning of it? Why is it described as "leftover,"

bearing "a trace of gilt lettering high on its false façade"? What is it that finally distracts the wandering cowboy-like "someone" from trying to decipher the gilt lettering?

3. Note that "deep into autumn" with "the nights gaining ground on the days" the narrator finds it curious that the "building of indeterminate function looms taller than before, or, more likely, it's simply that everything else seems shrunken and shriveled with aging." Why, then, is the narrator confused by "this human weeping...what we are hearing now," and why does he add "surely it is all like nothing we ever expected to witness or hear"?

"Fool's Paradise"

1. How does this story connect with the others and who is the narrator? Again, is he the main character or just an observer? How do we know that Hadley Graves, the narrator's wife, did get around to praising her husband for "The Eighth World of Royden Taul"?

2. What does the narrator mean when he remarks, half way through the story, "we'd been there, to the Heart of America, and yet we hadn't"?

3. Why does the narrator decide not to tell the investigating sheriff about the encounters he and Bye Johnson had with the "downhill geezer"? What does he mean when he says "It's what's real that absorbs me, gentlemen, absorbs and appalls me, both – why, there's the curse, come to think of it"? Also, when he adds that the curse of the geezer "was hardly a matter for the sheriff, but rather a private, moral matter—what I've called a road sign of the spirit"? Why is he unable to explain even to Laurel Leroux about Bye's death and the letter from him "that was probably never sent" to her? What imagery is conjured up for possible comparison at the end of this story?

"Gleanings"

1. This story opens with Graves being uncertain whether one of the gargoyles which decorate the wall of the church he walks by daily is missing, and in the third paragraph "he could not be sure, but it sounded like the music of a band that he was hearing." How many times during this story does he encounter something he cannot be sure of before the story ends with "though of this, of

course, he cannot be sure"? Did this ending surprise you, or were you waiting for it?

2. What do you make of the final section of this story, which begins with "most of the time one sees perfectly normal men and women passing by the Station House..."? Is this a reminder for us of the stranger in the streets whom, earlier in the story, he had taken to looking for and sometimes following? What do you make of the relationship between the two, particularly since the stranger is described as a man "whose whole demeanor is given to indecision and introspection"?

3. Why does Graves change the name of the dog, whom he early on realizes to be "the last great love of his life," from Woolly to Willy? Whether this decision is conscious or not, is there a clue when we look back on the second story, "Family Album"?

"The Westward Inn"

1. Where is this story first alluded to and briefly described in an unflattering clause? What does the author say about its title in the preceding story? Which of the titles he considers do you think best, or is it really necessary to choose?

2. What do you make of the first-person narrator's "stirrings of a vague regret" when, near the end of the story, he discovers that his watch has stopped? On the subject of time, why do the Inn's patrons, mostly elderly or "well along in late middle age," find it useful to divide "the era of the Westward Inn" into its "B.B. and A.B." years, signifying "Before" or "After" the "Brother"? Who is this "brother," and what is his nature, especially when compared to that of his brother Alberto?

3. What does the narrator-protagonist mean when he says, at the end, "I dwell upon that sea of stains until I'm gone"? Why does Alberto's brother, on the subject of the parking lot stains, rage near the end "Keep these spots! These spots they are good!"?

"The Roads Around Perdido"

1. This story, which can be referred to as the "title story," was introduced in

the fourth story, where it is described as a ghost town and given its name. But is there also a reminder near the end of "The Westward Inn," the story which precedes it? Did you find the reference to "the road that led south out of La Junta"? What does Perdido mean in Spanish? And also, La Junta?

2. The point of view in this story is worth discussing: The narrator, never identified, is addressing the reader as "you" throughout, while referring to himself as "I" or "me." Yet this narrator seems to be omniscient, for how else could this narrator be foretelling the future at the end of this story? Who is it?

3. Recalling the "flashbacks" we encountered in the second story (and there are some longer ones in "Gleanings," you may have noticed), which of the three sections of "The Roads Around Perdido" might be considered a flashback? During this long flashback, what is the significance of the protagonist confusing the Sierra Escondida ("hidden") with the name he employs, Sierra Encantada ("enchanted")? What does he discover—and who is the barking dog—when he awakes at the foot of the mountain after his long hike?

"Report on the Hadleyburg Renaissance"

1. Doesn't this story read like narrative fiction instead of a "report," as it is labeled in the title? What is one exception? The four footnotes would more commonly be found in a report, surely, but here, taken in order, don't they tell a story of their own? Who is fleeing from what in this story within the story, and how does he justify his flight? The wife, Hadley Graves, speaks of it as "something unfinished," in the second story, and its author, Charles Graves, speaks of it later in the sixth story, "Gleanings." What does he say about it?

2. Does this story seem to be finished, or is it suddenly interrupted when it ends? Given the nature of the interruption, could our answer go either way?

3. The bulk of this story may seem fantastic, but are there moments which might be considered as visionary? Consider, for example, the words of the leader "with light in his eyes," perhaps one of those who "foresaw in the moment the dawning of a new era":

"Nothing," he exclaimed, "has ever lifted our standard of living as much as the mutual goodwill of those who are doing the living."

"Dilsey's Story"

1. This story is not forecast by any of the first nine, and yet, can you find the place where it could tie into the sixth story, "Gleanings," providing Graves with a "second chance" with an event which may have been a "turning point" for him?

2. Also, could not "Dilsey's Story" be considered an elaboration on the final three sentences of the story which precedes it?

3. Consider the response of Graves to the boy at the schoolyard playground, on a weekend, who asks "where do you get a dog like that?" Graves seems to consider before he answers: "You just have to be lucky. Sometimes it's just a matter of fate, you know." Is he joking, or is he serious? One page earlier the vet who has examined Dilsey says "You sure can pick 'em," to which Graves explains "But it was she who salvaged me...a gift of fate, I think of it." Are there events in this book which might qualify Graves to speak about fate? What contemporary school of thought, or philosophy, maintains that in its view of "the human condition" we are all subject to fate, or chance (a view as old as that of the Book of Ecclesiastes, in the Old Testament, they sometimes like to point out)?

CPSIA information can be obtained
at www.ICGtesting.com
Printed in the USA
FFHW022331230919
55174401-60899FF